WYCLIFFE AND THE HOUSE OF FEAR

WYCLIFFE
AND THE
HOUSE OF FEAR

W. J. Burley

ST. MARTIN'S PRESS ❧ NEW YORK

Library of Congress Cataloging-in-Publication Data

Burley, W. J. (William John)
Wycliffe and the house of fear / by W.J. Burley.
    p.   cm.
ISBN 0-312-14080-0
1. Wycliffe, Charlie (Fictitious character)—Fiction.
2. Police—England—West Country—Fiction.
I. Title.
PR6052.U647W885   1996
823'.914—dc20   95-30037   CIP

First published in Great Britain by Victor Gollancz

First U.S. Edition: January 1996
10 9 8 7 6 5 4 3 2 1

To Muriel, without whose collaboration and constructive criticism there would have been no books

Prologue

Extract from the *Cornish Gazette* dated 15 June

Well-known Cornishwoman in Yachting Tragedy

Mrs Julia Kemp of Kellycoryk was lost overboard while sailing with her husband and a friend about two miles south of St Anthony Head on Tuesday afternoon. Mr Kemp was at the tiller of his eighteen-foot yacht *Winifred*, and Miss Clare Jordan, a friend of the family, was in the well of the boat with him. Mrs Kemp had chosen a position on the foredeck, her back propped against the mast. The weather was fine, and with a following breeze conditions were ideal.

When they were almost due south of St Anthony Head they were passed at some distance by a container ship heading up channel. The turbulence of the wash from this vessel caused the *Winifred* to pitch and roll and although Mr Kemp shouted to his wife she failed to be warned in time and fell into the sea where she was lost to sight almost at once.

Mr Kemp launched the life raft, lowered the foresail, and started his outboard motor. A distress rocket brought other craft to the scene and the search continued, to be joined later by a search-and-rescue helicopter; all to no avail.

Mrs Kemp, the mother of two teenage children, was an accomplished painter and for several years was prominent in the cultural life of the county with a special concern for the visual arts.

Chapter One

Monday 3 May (Five years later)

Roger Kemp was working in his library; a pleasant room, square and high, with bookshelves reaching to a generous frieze. There was a richly moulded cornice and the ceiling sported an improbable selection of plaster fruit and flowers, but every plaster surface was encrusted with the grime of years.

Roger worked at a big table littered with books, papers and charts, in the middle of which a black cat curled asleep, sleek and slim as a serpent.

Five minutes past eight on a sunny morning; Roger had been at work since six. An electric radiator close to his chair fended off the early morning chill. For at all times, even in summer, the old house was never free of a chilly dampness, and year by year Roger watched while eroding moulds made inroads on wood and plaster, paper and fabrics.

He consoled himself with the idea, and sometimes believed, that in the long run, whatever happened to Kellycoryk, to him, or to the family they would all survive in his *History of the Kemps of Kellycoryk*, a record of almost five centuries of industry and endurance.

Sometimes he wished that he could shut himself away in this room, a scholarly recluse. The Kemps were Catholics and, as a young man, Roger had been tempted by the cloistered life. The obligation of chastity would have troubled him little, yet through some element of the perverse the course of his life seemed to have been moulded, even warped, by women.

A tap at the door and his sister, Agnes, called, shrill and peremptory, 'Breakfast in ten minutes!'

The black cat raised its head, fiercely alert, watching Roger with yellow-green eyes. Roger reached out a reassuring hand. 'It's all right, Coryk.'

He returned to his manuscript, fingering the pages, and read aloud from the passage he had just written. Then he addressed the cat. 'Will anybody ever read that, Coryk? Will any publisher ever give it a chance?'

The cat showed no particular interest but when Roger got up from his chair, in a single clean leap Coryk was on the floor at his feet. They moved to one of the twin windows and Roger stood looking out. A large pond, almost a lake, with rushes at the margins, separated the house from a wilderness of laurel and rhododendron. Beyond the wilderness he could see the grey roofs of the cottages in the cove and the sea beyond, broad and empty and sparkling.

He caught sight of his reflection in the window, distorted by imperfections in the old glass. They seemed to exaggerate the drooping eyelids, the prominent nose and sagging jowls, the distinctive Kemp features which became more pronounced with age. Now, looking at his own reflection, he thought he saw his father's face.

'Breakfast, Coryk!' The cat paced him out of the room and down the dim passage to the kitchen. The family had their meals in the kitchen where an Aga maintained a cosy warmth even in the coldest weather. It was a large, bare room with adzed beams, cream-washed walls and a floor of slate slabs laid over with sisal matting. A naked bulb suspended from a central beam competed with the greenish-grey daylight which filtered through the parboiled glass.

On the big table, which was only partly covered by a cloth, there were packets of breakfast foods with a selection of crockery and cutlery from which people helped themselves. On the Aga, along with a saucepan of stock, was a rack of toast, a jug of milk, and a giant-sized blue-enamelled coffee pot with a chipped lid.

Crispin, Roger's son by his first wife, and Agnes were already at table. Crispin was nineteen, dark haired, pale faced, quiet and withdrawn. He was removing the top from his boiled egg with the same precision and concentration which he brought to everything he did. He looked up as his father entered, his eyes as limpid and guileless as a spaniel's. Roger never ceased to wonder what went on behind those eyes and at the genetic lottery which had given him two children so alike in looks and so different in temperament. Isobel, Crispin's sister, was a reincarnation of her dead mother.

Agnes said, 'Your egg is in the saucepan, it will be boiled hard by now.'

Agnes had a feminine version of the Kemp features, the drooping eyelids and dark colouring, but the heavy jowls were less in evidence.

Before retrieving his egg Roger went through to the old wash place and came back with a saucer of cat food which he put on the floor beside his chair. Only then did he fetch his egg from the stove.

'Isobel not down yet? She'll be late for work.' Isobel worked at a health food shop in Truro.

'She's on holiday this week and next.' Agnes said it as though the very fact was a personal affront.

Three or four years older than her brother, Agnes saw herself as a self-sacrificing spinster, trapped by her sense of duty into dependence.

Roger prepared his egg while Agnes sipped her coffee, continuing to hold the cup to her lips with both hands while watching him over the rim. For no apparent reason there was tension in the air.

Roger spoke to his son: 'Last evening I was up at the Northern Garden taking a look at your work, Crispy. You must have cleared nearly an acre; and Frank has made a good job of the roof of the old lodge . . .' His voice trailed off as he realized that even this modest show of enthusiasm was somehow out of place.

Crispin was attending classes in horticulture and, with the help of a part-time employee, he was clearing an area in the Northern Garden in the hope of starting a commercial nursery.

Agnes said, 'You'll need capital for glasshouses or plastic tunnels or whatever they are; then there's equipment, as well as fertilizers, plants, seeds . . . Where do you think the money's coming from?'

Roger ventured, 'I think we might manage it.'

Agnes ignored him. 'Of course there wouldn't be any problem if Bridget would show a spark of interest. After all, she is your stepmother and she wouldn't miss a few thousands, but I'm afraid you'll have to wait a long time if that's what you're counting on.'

There was a sound of movement from the back premises and Bridget herself came in, followed by a slightly overweight Labrador. She wore a half-length fawn suede coat with trousers, and a waterproof hat over her red hair. She was petite, delicate as porcelain, but she looked flushed with health and vitality. The dog, after a preliminary reconnoitre, settled in front of the Aga.

Coryk, tail erect, back arched, hissed so that Roger had to soothe him.

Bridget said, 'Timmy and I have had a lovely walk, it's a wonderful morning and the gorse is unbelievable . . . the colour, and the scent!'

Two years ago Roger had married Bridget, the daughter of a shrewd and prosperous businessman who had promptly died of a heart attack, leaving her in charge of an expanding and profitable business in the leisure industry.

'Goodness, it's warm in here!' Bridget slipped out of her coat. Underneath she wore a gaily patterned blouse like a sunburst in the gloom.

Agnes said, 'There are eggs and there's toast.'

Bridget looked about her and decided, 'No, I think I'll have some muesli; I need to lose weight.'

Agnes, her eyes on Bridget, buttered a piece of toast. She seemed to be waiting, and when Bridget was settled she said, 'We've just been talking about Crispin's scheme for the nursery. It's really a question of where he's going to get the capital.' She spoke as though the business had been a subject for family discussion.

Roger stopped in the act of chewing a mouthful of toast, and Crispin looked at Agnes in disbelief.

But Bridget was saved from comment. Isobel, wearing her dressing gown, drifted in. She rubbed her eyes like a sleepy child and asked in a plaintive voice, 'What time is it?'

Agnes said, 'There's a clock on the wall.'

It was true that in features and colouring Isobel resembled her brother, but she was a striking girl; a mass of almost black hair accentuated her pallor and her lips appeared dramatically red. As her late mother had once remarked, 'Like blood on snow.'

She pulled out a chair and sat down, stretching and yawning. 'It feels like the middle of the night.' She reached for a bowl and for the cornflakes packet but realizing that she would have to get up for the milk she abandoned the idea.

Instead she sat back in her chair and announced, 'Mother spoke to me last night.'

Roger felt that he was about to be drawn into some kind of vortex. He said, 'What on earth are you talking about?'

'It was rather marvellous, actually.' Isobel was becoming animated. 'A little group – just seven of us; we've been meeting for three or four weeks with a medium called Teresa from St Endel Churchtown. She tried to make contact with Mother twice before and last night it worked.' Isobel's manner was brisk and brittle.

Crispin was watching his sister uneasily but no one spoke, and she went on, 'It was Mother's voice, just like having her in the room.'

Agnes said, 'You don't remember your mother's voice.'

'Of course I do! I was sixteen, for God's sake! I remember everything about her, how she looked, how she smiled, how she dressed . . . You remember, don't you, Crispin?'

Crispin said nothing and the ticking of the clock was left to fill the silence.

Then Isobel began again. 'Mother was very upset. She said, "I've longed to speak to you, Isobel, but I can't do it unless you help me. You must try to reach me as I struggle to reach you . . . There are things I want you to know, but it's very difficult to break through –"'

The girl spoke in a low, tense monotone when quoting her mother's words but broke off to speak normally immediately afterwards. 'That was all . . . It was like being cut off on the telephone . . . Of course I shall go on trying; I shan't give up now. Teresa, as a favour, has agreed to try again tomorrow night.'

It was Bridget who spoke finally. She sounded remote and judicial. 'Of course, what you do and what you believe, Isobel, is up to you, but before you are led to do something you might regret I should make sure that you are not being exploited by this woman.'

Isobel looked at her with a glazed expression. 'That's what I would expect you to say.'

The arrival of the daily maid put further discussion on hold.

She came in through the back and stood in the doorway, a young girl from the cove, Jane Clemens; fresh, if inclined to be raw, with a manner which made it clear that she was nobody's doormat. She looked at Agnes. 'Where do you want me to start?'

Agnes said, 'Surely you know by now. It's Monday, so you change the beds.'

The girl shrugged. 'It's all the same to me.'

As she crossed the room there was a momentary exchange of glances between her and Crispin, not lost on Agnes.

Wycliffe looked out of the window of the living room at a tranquil, sunlit sea, at the slow ripples that produced a lace of foam on the shingle, and decided that they had come to the right place. A little way up the shallow valley, Kellycoryk House was visible between the trees, the low pitched roof with over-hanging eaves seemed to rise out of a shrubby wilderness.

Wycliffe was convalescent; overwork, a bad bout of influenza followed by bronchitis and a touch of pleurisy had kept him out of circulation for several weeks. Now, before returning to the treadmill, on medical advice and on orders from his chief, he was having a holiday 'away from it all'.

'Away from it all' materialized into this cottage, one of a dozen or so, stone-built and slate-roofed, scattered in an irregular crescent about the margin of a tiny, rocky cove facing south into Veryan Bay. The Wycliffes had visions of walks along the Cornish cliffs, through the lanes and over the moors.

A stream divided the little community into two, but it was reunited by a bridge (Max Wt 2T). Beyond the bridge the stream spread out and all but lost itself in the shingle on the shore.

There was no sound, and no sign of life anywhere.

The choice had been Helen's, made because she had discovered that the name, Kellycoryk, is Cornish for elf wood or rather, wood elf; also because the cove was managed by Coast and Country, a leisure company with a good reputation in the business. Helen's best decisions were often based on a nice blend of whimsy and calculation.

Half-past ten; they had made a leisurely trip. Helen was inspecting the accommodation and finding it to her liking. There was electricity, with provision for a wood fire in the living room.

There were two bedrooms, an adequate bathroom and kitchen; a TV and a telephone.

Mrs Moyle, the woman who supervised the lets, lived with her family in one of the other cottages. Thin and wiry, her grey hair cut short, she had a youngish face betrayed by fine wrinkles on her upper lip. She was polite but distant.

Helen said, 'Do all the cottages belong to the leisure company?'

'They don't any of them belong; they're only leased from the estate.'

'So the cove is still part of the Kellycoryk estate?'

'Like it always was.'

Wycliffe tried his hand. 'Does anybody live in the big house?'

'Live there? Of course they do. The Kemp family live there like they always did.' She had no intention of being drawn into gossip.

Helen, with her taste for Victorian novelists, had mentally labelled her Mrs Tightlip.

Helen said, 'Well, there's nothing we need do here. What about a walk to the village, buy a few things and perhaps get some lunch?'

Mrs Moyle volunteered, 'If you want lunch, Jack Sara's wife at the New Inn is a good cook.'

They walked along the road they had driven earlier; it was overhung by a low cliff and there was a notice, 'Crumbling cliffs. Beware of falling stones.'

'What are we supposed to do? Dodge?'

The road rose steeply to surmount a promontory which separated the cove from the larger inlet and village of Porthendel; a broad stubby headland, pushed raggedly into the sea.

Wycliffe said, 'It's called Jacob's Head, according to the map.'

Down the further slope they came to the village where a crooked jetty defended the tiny harbour.

Old fish lofts had found other uses: one was a café, another a picture gallery, while two more had become desirable waterfront residences. The Wycliffes strolled happily, not saying much; words that were spoken usually came in answer to the other's thoughts. Wycliffe reflected, We are an old married couple, becoming smug; because we like it that way.

They turned up a narrow, steep slope into the village square.

It was not really a square but a triangle at the junction of three roads, itself on a slope. A few visitors, in pairs or in family groups, drifted around the square, down to the waterfront and back again, while a café, with tables outside, served morning coffee to those who wished to take the weight off their feet.

There were several shops; a newsagent's on one corner was also the post office; no company shops. The New Inn had a board outside: 'Lunches 12.00–2.00.'

'We'll come back to all that.'

They were attracted by 'Clare Jordan's Old Curiosity Shop'. At first sight it was an ordinary little shop selling bric-à-brac, but the bygones were of more than average quality. Clare Jordan, whoever she was, had an eye for small pieces of china and glass, and the knack of displaying them.

Helen said, 'See those dogs?'

She was looking at a pair of china 'comforter' dogs, white glazed, with spots or splashes of copper lustre. Recently Helen had developed a taste for that kind of thing, presumably in line with her Victorian reading. 'They would look good on the kitchen shelf. I wonder what she wants for them. Shall we ask?'

They could see two women in the shop; one of them, presumably Clare Jordan herself, was seated on a chair by a door leading to an adjoining room. She was in her middle forties, well preserved, with a bony physique innocent of curves. The other, standing by her, was a thin, pale girl with a mop of dark hair. She wore a jade-green tunic which barely reached her thighs and black leggings. The effect was dramatic.

As Wycliffe opened the door the older woman was saying, her voice raised, 'You have become totally unbalanced about your mother, Isobel. Obsessed! If you—' She broke off on the instant and turned to her customers. The girl however continued to stare at her and Wycliffe was made uncomfortable by those coldly appraising eyes.

Helen opened negotiations for her dogs. The woman quite recovered her poise and her business sense, while the girl turned her back on all three of them, waiting for the strangers to go.

It was obvious that the confrontation or whatever it was would be resumed when they left, and it was not long before they did, Helen, with her dogs snug in a cardboard box.

Helen said, 'We interrupted something.'

They decided on a drink before lunch and went to the New Inn where they joined a group around the bar. The landlord said, 'Lunch? If you want lunch somebody will be along in a few minutes.'

At one end of the bar there was a group of tables railed off. No slot machines, no pool table, no canned music; Helen purred, and they took their drinks to one of the tables behind the rail.

Others began to arrive and several tables were occupied. A plump woman in a white coat put up a chalkboard. 'Meal of the Day: Chicken with mushrooms and courgettes; sauté potatoes. Apple pie with Cornish clotted cream.'

Colours nailed to the mast. No compromise, no options.

'Shall we have a half-bottle of something?'

'Look!' Helen nodded towards a couple just seating themselves at a table for two in a far corner of the bar. 'The woman from the dog shop and the girl. They seemed to have settled their quarrel, if it was one.'

Wycliffe studied the pair with interest. 'From the look of them I wouldn't bet on it.'

When the plump woman came to take their order Helen asked, 'Who's the girl with the woman from the antique shop?'

The landlady looked across at the pair and smiled. 'Striking girl, isn't she? Isobel Kemp, from Kellycoryk, Roger Kemp's daughter by his first wife. And just like her mother; a real beauty she was. Clare Jordan is related to them somehow.'

Wycliffe was beginning to enjoy himself. He loved to find out about people. Even as a child, when taken somewhere new, it had intrigued him to discover people of whose existence he had known nothing. He would watch them with a sense of wonder and afterwards he would think of them going on with their lives when he wasn't there. Helen said that it was this inquisitive streak that had made him a policeman.

After their meal they did their shopping and Wycliffe bought a local history book on Kellycoryk and the Kemps.

The afternoon was overcast and misty so that Roger, in his library, was working by artificial light. He brooded over a letterbook which held correspondence between his great-grandfather and the Tehidy estate. The crabbed script frequently defeated him and in any case his mind was elsewhere. Isobel's absurd tale of her medium troubled him and he tried to tell himself that it was nothing more than another of the girl's odd whims.

At forty-six Roger felt that time had stolen a march on him. It seemed that the transition from vaguely hopeful and aspiring youth to despairing and stressful middle age had been visited upon him unjustly. At times he felt like some defenceless sea creature who puts out an exploratory tentacle only to have it bitten off.

The telephone rang and he picked it up.

'Is that you, Roger . . . ? It's Clare. Is it safe to talk?'

'I suppose so.' His manner lacked enthusiasm.

'Isobel came to the shop this morning. At first she pretended she wanted to buy a present for Agnes's birthday but it was obvious that she was out to make trouble. She's been going to seances and she says she's had a message from Julia.'

Roger felt the tension rising and his fingers gripped the telephone. 'I know.'

'Has she said anything about us?'

'About *us*?'

His emphasis on the word seemed to offend her. 'Don't play with me, Roger! Yes, about us! She as good as asked how much you gave me to set me up in the business.'

'But that's nonsense!'

'All right, but in almost the same breath she started to talk of discovering what really happened when her mother died. I mean, it was blatant. To get her out of the shop I took her to lunch at the pub but it made no difference. She said that she expected to know more when her mother spoke to her again.'

Roger was barely articulate. 'But she can't—'

Clare cut him short. 'I'm worried, Roger, and we've got to talk – not over the telephone. I'll expect you this evening.'

Roger was cut off. He replaced his phone and stared at it as though he had been bitten. Then he held his breath; it was a trick he had learned in childhood. When there was something that he did not want to think about he would hold his breath until the pressure in his head was almost unbearable, then when he started to breathe again he could usually think of something else. It had become a survival technique.

*   *   *

The Wycliffes were back in their cottage in the cove. Helen was arranging the kitchen to her liking while he sat in a wicker chair by the window of the living room, leafing through his book on the Kemps and Kellycoryk. It turned out to be one of those little gems of local history, published on a shoe-string.

He learned that the family had arrived at Kellycoryk at about the time when Henry VIII of England and Francis I of France were displaying like peacocks on the Field of the Cloth of Gold. As Catholics, the Kemps of Kellycoryk, unlike some of their namesakes, had the good sense to keep their heads down during the religious upheavals. But there must have been some bad moments with the influential, time-serving Trevanions almost next door at Caerhays.

The Wycliffes' cottage was sideways on to the cove so that from his window Wycliffe could look down to the sea or up the valley to Kellycoryk House. The mist was like a thin veil; it did not exclude the view but added a certain fuzziness like a slightly out-of-focus lens.

He was thinking about the contemporary Kemps and becoming increasingly interested in that gloomy-looking house almost hidden in a seeming wilderness.

'I think I'll take a look around the cove. You don't feel like coming?'

'It's not worth it; I've got things to do and I'm quite happy here.'

Their cottage was nearest the shore and he had to pass three or four others before reaching the bridge. A group of children, presumably on their way home from school, were playing by the stream – three girls and a boy. The scene reminded him of those idealized versions of rural life by Victorian painters. Two of the little girls wore skirts.

On the other side of the stream he should have followed the road by the crumbling cliffs, but he looked up the valley towards the gates of Kellycoryk and decided to take a closer look. In fact, there were no gates, only a pair of massive granite gateposts and a well-weathered notice: 'Kellycoryk Estate. Strictly Private.' There was a gatehouse, but the roof had fallen in and the window frames were empty. A weedy drive, just wide enough for a car, disappeared between the encroaching laurels.

There was no sound anywhere except the gentle rippling of

the stream and the breaking of lilliputian waves over the shingle
in the cove. Even the children were silent. So far Wycliffe had
only seen the roof of the house and he wanted a closer view.
After a couple of twists the drive opened out and he was surprised to find a virtual lake between him and the house. The
surface was largely covered by a green scum and rushes were
taking over the shallows, but what he had come to see was the
house; and there it was in clear view.

It was not large as country houses go, a single block of two
storeys with dormers above, and here too there was evidence of
neglect and decay. In places the stucco-facing had flaked away
exposing underlying brickwork, and rampant ivy reached to the
windows of the first floor. From where he stood he could see,
on the east side of the building, an area of low scrub from which,
here and there, broken walls emerged, presumably the site of
an earlier house.

While he stood there a car, a blue Mondeo Estate, appeared
from around the side of the house, skirted the lake and came
towards him. Instinctively he dodged into the laurels, and then
felt foolish. The car passed, and he saw a woman at the wheel.
For an instant their eyes met and he had a glimpse of red hair
and the impression of a beautiful, doll-like face.

Gradually the sound of the car died away but he could still
hear it a couple of minutes later as it climbed the slope to the
village.

He walked back to the bridge; the mist was thickening into
fog; the children had gone indoors, and he could no longer see
the sea.

Crispin got into bed, pulled the bedclothes over him and
switched off his bedside lamp. His curtains were undrawn, the
mists had cleared with the turn of the tide and through his
window he could see the stars. As his eyes accommodated he
could pick out the familiar objects in his room.

This time each night before he fell asleep was important to
Crispin. Once he had closed his bedroom door he began to feel
secure – not against any physical danger but against the more
subtle threat of emotional intrusion. In all the encounters of his
day Crispin took refuge behind a mask of placidity, usually
interpreted by others as coldness or indifference. But that mask

was his defence against intimacy of any sort; the cut and thrust of ordinary relationships scared him and he could not bear to contemplate the consequences of becoming involved.

Crispin had constructed for himself a tiny world where contacts were few and life was predictable. The boundaries of Kellycoryk defined its physical limits and he went outside them only of sheer necessity.

But sex had become a problem, strangely disturbing, even menacing, to his world. It was solved to some extent, almost accidentally, by the girl who came to help with the cleaning, and encounters with her, two or three times a week, entered into the routine of his days. But there could be no doubt that they profoundly disturbed that uncertain equilibrium he had so painfully contrived.

Drifting off to sleep he was aware of a slight sound and he saw his bedroom door opening.

'Are you asleep, Crispy?' It was Isobel. She was in her nightdress and she came to stand beside his bed. 'I want to talk to you.'

Crispin dreaded this approach; usually it meant that his sister was about to involve him in something of which he wanted to know nothing. 'Can't it wait until tomorrow?'

'No.' She pulled back his bedclothes and got in beside him.

He could feel her naked thigh against his and he moved away.

'Don't go away, I'm cold. In any case, you'll fall out the other side.'

'We shouldn't be here like this.'

'Why not? When we were children we used to sleep in the same bed.'

'That was different. We're not children now.'

She made an irritable movement. 'Are you going to let me talk or not?'

He said nothing and she went on, 'What I said about Mother I almost think was true, Crispy. She really seemed to speak to me and I believe there are things she wants to tell me.'

'What things?' The words were forced from him.

'I don't know yet. I hope there will be other sessions and that she will speak again.' She added after a moment, 'But I can guess what it's about.'

He was disturbingly aware of her body and his emotions were

wildly confused. He was desperate to put an end to the situation. 'How can you if she didn't tell you?'

'Never mind, I think I know . . .' She broke off. 'Do you remember all that happened around the time Mother died?'

'Of course I remember it!'

'Did you believe what they told the police?'

He said, bleakly, 'I suppose I believed it – yes.'

'Who was on the boat besides Mother and Father?'

'Clare was on the boat.'

Crispin was troubled by the way in which she had once more succeeded in putting him at a disadvantage. Now he was being subjected to some sort of test. It had always been the same. She would cross-question him, catch him out, and so re-establish or confirm a certain ascendancy which she had had over him since infancy.

Isobel demanded, 'Where was I the day Mother died?'

A momentary hesitation. 'You were away on a school trip somewhere. You were supposed to be away all that week.'

'Yes, and Aunt Agnes was staying with her friend in Torquay, so there was you, and Mother and Father and, of course, Clare was still living with us then.'

'Yes.'

Isobel took a deep breath. 'It was a Tuesday when it happened so you were at school. Were they quarrelling the night before?'

'I don't know.'

'What was she like next morning – before you went to school?'

Crispin spoke very slowly as though each word came with difficulty. 'I didn't see her. You know how it was; Clare used to get the breakfast when Agnes was away.'

'Yes. Now about what they told the police; they said that Clare was in the well of the boat with Father who was at the tiller, but that Mother was on the foredeck – why?'

'I think they said she wanted to sunbathe.'

'Yes, she wanted to sunbathe!' Isobel was derisive. 'Mother would never sunbathe; she was too worried about her skin; she had to be, because she was pale like me.'

Crispin said nothing.

'It would have been so simple.' Isobel sounded thoughtful.

'What would?' The question seemed to be forced from him.

'I don't know. How did Clare manage to buy her shop not long after Mother died?'

'Clare had her shop before Mother died.'

'But she was renting it as a lock-up and she lived with us. When Mother died she bought it, then later went to live in the rooms over the shop. She couldn't have done it on her own; where did she get the money from?'

He almost shouted, 'I don't know and I don't want to know, Isobel!'

Isobel ignored him. 'Anyway, Clare was settled in her own shop and after two or three years Father married Bridget.'

They were quiet for a few moments; Crispin was tense, waiting, when Isobel burst out, 'It's this bloody house; that's what it comes back to.'

'The house?'

'Yes, the house, this place . . . It cripples us all. I get to hate the very sight and smell of it . . . I wish it would fall down, burn down – anything so that we could get out and live like other people. But Father is a Kemp and so we have to skimp and scheme and pretend . . .' She broke off. 'And you're just as bad, with your bloody nursery; as though, even if it worked, it could make any real difference.'

Crispin was silent; he lay rigid and still. There was a brief interval of quiet then Isobel bounced up in the bed and put her arms around him. 'Now I've got that off my chest you can warm me up before I go back to my own bed.'

He struggled to free himself and she laughed, a rare occurrence with Isobel. 'What's the matter? Are you afraid you might be tempted to rape me or something? It would be different if I were Jane Clemens, wouldn't it?'

'Isobel! Stop it!' The words were hissed at her, and he was gripping her arms so tightly that she was frightened, and became quiet at once. 'All right, I'm listening.'

He said nothing for a moment and when he did speak his voice was controlled. 'I want you to drop all this, it can do no good. You've no idea what you are doing – no idea!' He seemed to have difficulty in finding words and there was another pause before he added, 'You will end up by . . .' Again he broke off, then finished lamely, 'You will make things worse.'

She was uneasy and, feeling slightly foolish, she took refuge in a childish retort. 'That's what you think!' And she slipped out of bed and was gone.

Left alone, Crispin lay rigid, every muscle taut, fingers and toes clenched, head throbbing.

Chapter Two

The morning was clear and bright and fresh. The Wycliffes were enjoying a holiday breakfast, semi-lethal, with an egg and a sausage.

From where he sat, Wycliffe was looking out of the window at the sunlit sea. 'Well, what's our programme for the day?'

Helen said, 'I thought we might walk the coast path to Portloe, Kiberick, and the Nare. I think we could probably get lunch in Veryan.'

'It sounds like a lot of miles.'

Helen was dismissive. 'Nonsense, Charles!'

Like most of Helen's plans, it worked; lovely cliff scenery, an abundance of spring wild flowers, and the delight of Portloe where they had coffee in a restaurant almost overhanging the cove and watched a fishing boat being winched up the beach. Then on to Kiberick, and Veryan for lunch. After that they had a less spectacular but pleasant trudge back through the lanes to St Endel Churchtown, little more than a mile inland from Porthendel.

In a dry-stone wall opposite the church a pair of ornamental gateposts marked what must once have been the imposing northern entrance to Kellycoryk. Now the only barrier was a rickety farm gate. Near the gate a substantial little building, with shuttered windows, must at one time have been a lodge.

Helen, arms on the gate, looking over, said, 'Somebody's been working in there – clearing the ground. I wonder if they're going in for reclamation.'

Over a considerable area the ground had been cleared and a start had been made digging out roots. The clearance had uncovered a track leading from the gateway into the wilderness beyond.

'What's left of the original drive.'

Helen said, 'There must still be a way through. Let's take a look.'

It was a waste of time to argue and in any case Wycliffe's curiosity would overcome his ingrained conformity. At least they managed to open the gate and avoid the indignity of climbing over.

Once out of the clearing they were treading a narrow path through a mixed jungle of rhododendron and camellia with frequent woodland trees, some well established, others in the thrusting sapling stage. Two centuries ago a garden had been carved out of the wood; now, slowly but surely, the wood was reclaiming its own.

At intervals they glimpsed broken walls and remnants of buildings which must once have been features in an ornamental park. The path they were following was largely notional, broken at intervals by sudden inexplicable changes of level, and from time to time there were muddy patches. Here and there the burgeoning growth had been cut back to maintain some sort of passage.

Wycliffe said, 'Don't you think we've had enough?'

'Let's see if we can reach the stream.'

Away to their left they could hear running water and the path seemed to be making broadly in that direction. Then, abruptly, the stream was in front of them, swirling between constraining banks. There was a bridge, whose generous width defined the scale of the original drive, its ornamental balustrade now almost lost under matted ivy. On the other side, in a large clearing, there was a substantial house with outbuildings.

Faced with the alternative of turning back they crossed the bridge, which meant passing close to the house. A neatly painted notice set on a post read: '*Chylathva*. Beware of Jackals.'

A sizeable patch of ground to one side of the house was enclosed by chicken wire, and within it a dozen or so hens pecked and scratched and clucked in apparent contentment. Helen, once a keeper of chickens, said, 'White Leghorns.'

Near the front door of the house, at first unnoticed by the Wycliffes, a dark-haired young woman with a stick was bent double, poking away at what appeared to be a choked drain. She glanced up without special interest. 'Looking for somebody?'

Wycliffe said, 'We're trespassers. We are renting one of the cottages in the cove and we wondered if there was a way through.'

The woman – she was in her thirties – stood up and swept back trailing hair from her face with a bare arm. 'There's a way through if you follow the stream. It's true Roger doesn't like people about the place but he won't eat you.'

Helen said, 'What about the jackals?'

The woman grinned happily. 'That's Francis – Roger's brother, I live here with him and, like all the Kemps, he's never grown up.' She turned back to her drain. 'Anyway, there's a good track from here direct to the Porthendel road if you don't fancy the stream walk, but don't let Roger put you off.'

Wycliffe said, 'Nice woman.'

In fact now the going was much easier; they simply followed the course of the stream and a few minutes later they were in sight of the big house.

Ahead their way seemed blocked by a long run of low out-buildings with decaying roofs, but as they drew nearer they saw that a broad archway gave access to a yard with the house beyond. At this point, abruptly and noisily, the stream plunged through a large grating into an underground culvert and dis-appeared.

'It must go under the house and come out in the lake.'

'Surely we don't have to go through the house yard?'

'It looks as though we do.'

The yard was reasonably well paved, but the outbuildings, presumably the former stables and coach house, were in a ruin-ous state and there was rubbish everywhere, from a massive sofa with escaping stuffing, to an ancient powered mower, red with rust. A newish open shed with a corrugated asbestos roof at the east end of the yard provided cover for the blue Mondeo, a museum-piece Volvo, and a white Mini.

Helen said, 'Wouldn't you think they'd do something about tidying this up?'

There was no one about and they made their way around the east end of the house with the overgrown ruins of a former building on their left. Wycliffe, out of his recently acquired knowledge, said, 'The original Tudor house.'

It was as they came round to the front, in sight of the lake, that they saw a man: stocky build, tweed suit and flat cap – the very model of a country gentleman. He had his back to them, apparently watching ducks on the lake as they dipped, bottoms up, for food. At his feet, instead of the traditional retriever, a black cat performed its acrobatic and elegant toilet.

The man turned, saw them, and came over; he had the heavy features which seem to characterize some of the oldest families and altogether he could have been an intimidating individual but Wycliffe sensed at once that he was more nervous than they.

Wycliffe spoke first. 'Charles Wycliffe. I'm afraid that we're intruders, without much excuse other than interest. We are staying at one of the cottages in the cove and our curiosity about Kellycoryk got the better of us.'

There was an inarticulate response, not unfriendly, then, 'I'm Roger Kemp.' A wry smile. 'I take it you've come by the Long Drive. I know it's hard to believe, but in the twenties there was a carriage drive from the northern entrance all the way to the house.'

Wycliffe, an incurable catophile, stooped to stroke the cat but Kemp stopped him. 'I wouldn't if I were you; Coryk can be quite nasty with strangers.'

Wycliffe said, 'He seems very much attached to you.'

Kemp was pleased. 'Black cats and Kemps and Kellycoryk go together. The story is that a seventeenth-century ancestor was awakened by the first Coryk when his bed-hangings caught fire.' A shy smile. 'And to prove it we have a painting of that heroic Coryk with a badly singed tail.'

Wycliffe tried to develop the conversation. 'I've been reading a most interesting little book on the Kemps and Kellycoryk. Your house and family have a long and enthralling history behind them.'

For some reason the compliment was not well received. Kemp frowned. 'I'm afraid Miss Scott's book can scarcely be called history.'

It was Helen's turn to change the subject. 'Does the stream actually go under the house?'

'Not under the present house, no.' Kemp's manner had become decidedly less friendly. He looked at Wycliffe. 'It hadn't occurred to me, your name is unusual – you must be—'

'The policeman. I'm afraid so.'

Not for the first time in such circumstances Wycliffe wished that he had been born a Smith, a Jones or a Brown, but he would not have expected his identity to have had any significance for Kemp. In fact there was a decided drop in temperature and an awkward pause before the man said, 'I suppose you are down here on holiday?'

'Yes, a spring break.'

'Well, I can only wish you good day and a pleasant holiday.'

As they were making their way around the lake Wycliffe said, 'What came over him?'

Helen was in no doubt. 'An antipathy for policemen; it's not uncommon.'

But Wycliffe was following his own line. 'A strange man. Not the sort I would expect to have married two very attractive women.'

Helen, still smarting from Kemp's snub, said, 'You know next to nothing about his first wife; you may have glimpsed the second, though you can't even be sure of that.'

'You only have to look at the daughter. She didn't get her looks from her father.' He went on, 'Three Kemps: Isobel, we saw in the dog shop and the pub; Roger, we've just met, and I feel sure that the woman I saw driving the Mondeo was his second wife. Now we know there's a brother called Francis, who lives with a very pleasant young woman who clears drains.'

Helen couldn't help laughing. 'Is this some sort of game?'

'Call it a jigsaw puzzle. But there are pieces missing, and so far we haven't fitted in the lady of the china dogs.'

'Does she?'

'Oh, I think so. The landlady in the pub said she was a relative, and we interrupted a rather heated discussion between her and Isobel, something about Isobel's mother – that would be the first Mrs Kemp . . .' Wycliffe broke off, then added, 'It's just occurred to me that we don't know what happened to her – did she die? Or was there a divorce?'

'You'd better ask Kemp when you see him again.'

But Helen's sarcasm was lost on her husband. 'No, I need to be a bit more subtle than that.'

Helen looked at him with affection. 'After all these years you never cease to surprise me, Charles. What has got into you about these people?'

They left Kellycoryk and arrived at the cove. Evening comes early to these south-facing coves; although the sun still shone there was a muted quality to the light which reminded Wycliffe of his boyhood, of summer Sunday evenings in chapel.

Helen said, 'Look at my shoes . . . and your trousers! A shower, a sherry, and a meal. How about that?'

Roger watched the Wycliffes as they made their way around the lake and down the drive. He had made a fool of himself. He had got out of the habit of talking with strangers. And then to discover that this one was a policeman . . . He realized that Isobel's activities were worrying him more than he would admit, but to imagine that this man . . . That, at least, was nonsense.

He turned away from the lake and walked back to the house, paced by the cat. He made for his library and once there Coryk leapt on to the table and curled up amid the litter of papers. Roger sat in his padded chair, leaned back and stared at the ceiling, his favourite position for relaxation.

Above his head the ceiling was defaced by a pattern of cracks; a pattern he knew so well that he could have drawn it from memory. Yet he saw them differently at different times; sometimes as a branching tree, sometimes as a river delta, occasionally as similar to the lines of destiny which are supposed to occur in one's hands. Once, not long ago, he had dreamed that he was sitting in his chair looking up at those cracks when they started to widen, and at such a rate that before he could move to protect himself, with a great rending and crashing, the whole ceiling had collapsed, burying him under a mountain of rubble. Miraculously he was unhurt, but helplessly imprisoned.

He still shivered at the memory of that dream.

The gathering was in a private house. The room was lit only by the light which diffused through the curtains drawn across the bow window. Four women and two men sat around an oval dining table. Teresa, the medium, was at one end, Isobel at the other.

Teresa wore a gown of yellow silk which, even in the dim light, produced subtle and changing reflections. Her long, pale hands rested on the table but her face was not visible. She sat, slumped in her chair, with her head drooping, chin on chest;

only her dark hair with its central parting was clearly seen.

She spoke without lifting her head so that her voice sounded muffled. 'Tonight I shall not use either of my spirit guides. I shall try to communicate directly with the spirit of our departed sister. At our last meeting her distress and her anxiety to communicate were such that I feel able to rely on her co-operation to this unusual extent.'

There was an interval, then the medium's voice resumed. 'If you will now concentrate on her given name – Julia. Repeat the name Julia to yourselves, over and over again, and at the same time *will* her to be with us and to speak.'

A brief silence, then came the sound of stertorous breathing, a garbled flow of words or near words, then silence again. This sequence was repeated, but the second time it was interrupted by the striking of the church clock which was so close that they could hear the mechanical whirring and clacking which punctuated the eight strokes.

One of the men, whose bald head shone in the dim light, muttered, 'You should have thought of that, Margot,' and was shushed by the others. Teresa seemed unaffected. More garbled speech, then a different voice, clear and authoritative, demanded, 'Is Isobel here?'

Margot, a plump figure with mauve lights in her hair, prompted. 'Answer your mother, Isobel!'

'I'm here, Mother.' Isobel sounded self-conscious and uncertain. After an interval, during which the medium breathed deeply and slowly, the voice came again, but this time the tone was less peremptory. 'You must ask *them* questions, Isobel . . . Keep asking them. There are things I cannot tell you . . . You must find them out for yourself . . . I haven't much time . . .' She sounded breathless.

'I want to know exactly how you died, Mother.' There was a tremor in the girl's voice.

This time the silence was so long that it seemed there would be no response but it came at last though the voice was weak. 'You know *how* I died, Isobel.'

And that was all.

Teresa moved in her chair, sitting bolt upright, and she said in a tired voice, 'Did I make contact?'

There were murmurings of assent and approval.

Margot said, 'It was very successful, Teresa. Isobel should be grateful to you.' She got up from her chair and went to the window where she drew back the curtains. At the bottom of the garden the church tower with its clock rose above a tall yew hedge. The sun was setting and the tower was caught in an orange glow.

Margot, bustling, said, 'Let's move into the other room. I'm sure we all need a drink.'

Bridget Kemp was seated at her work table by the window. The curtains were undrawn and the window panes shone blankly against the darkness outside. The little digital clock registered five minutes past eleven. The desk lamp cast only a semi-circle of light out into the room so that most of it was in shadow. Bridget's tiny fingers seemed to dance over the keyboard of her word processor as a memorandum took shape on the screen.

'Inter-office memo to Ian Curtis from BK. 4.5.93.

'Reference: April returns. For the second month in succession, there are items for which the information provided is totally inadequate . . .'

Bridget took pleasure in most things that she did, not least in reminding her staff of their obligations and their dependence.

There was a gentle tap at the door and she turned to see Roger in his dressing gown coming into the room, manifestly unsure of his reception. Surely he didn't imagine . . . No! The thought was stillborn. She looked, to make sure that he was not followed by his cat.

'I hope I'm not disturbing you but I wanted a word . . . I could hear you tapping away, so I knew you were still at work.'

Bridget stood up and drew forward a chair as though for a visitor.

Roger wedged himself into a tub chair that was too small for him. His drooping lids and sagging jowls gave him the look of a grieving mastiff.

'I'm worried, Bridget.'

'Oh?' As though the fact came as a surprise. 'What about?'

'You know what about. About us, about the future, the estate – everything.'

Her attitude was that of a doctor with a difficult patient. 'Well, the remedy is in your own hands.'

He tried to shift in his chair but the chair moved with him and he looked ridiculous.

She went on, 'There's no way in which you will persuade me to spend money on this place chasing your dream, Roger. I've said that often enough, but you don't seem to understand that I mean it. You can't live on sentiment, even five centuries of it. But, apart from anything else, you don't even make use of the assets you have – for one thing, income from the farms could be doubled with proper management; and your brother lives off you, he pays no rent for a property which, renovated, and offered in the right market, could bring in a good income. Instead, you pay his council tax while he dabbles with his paints, producing stuff which no one could possibly buy, pretending that he's a neglected genius.'

'Francis got nothing under Father's will.'

Bridget made a dismissive gesture. 'Your father's will! Your father was a realist, Roger. He knew that the Kemp legend couldn't be sustained for much longer and it's obvious that he fully expected you to sell up. He made provision that if and when you decided or were forced to do so, Francis and the others would receive a proportion of the capital sum raised. I've told you, though I doubt if you believed me, that two years before the old man died he was putting out feelers about selling the place. It was common talk in the business. All the company is asking of you is a long lease which would be wholly in your favour.'

This, with variations, was more or less familiar ground, a sort of preamble to serious discussion; then Bridget broke into new territory: 'Now there is Isobel; if you allow her to go on the way she is going you may find yourself in another kind of trouble and that would do none of us any good.'

'I don't know what you mean.'

'I think you understand only too well.' The doll-like features and the blue eyes looked innocent of any possible threat, but the voice was hard.

Roger's gaze shifted around the room as though in search of inspiration while she watched him with total detachment.

The silence was absolute until broken by the distant barking of a dog.

She waited, unmoving, until Roger said, 'I suppose we could continue to live here?'

Bridget sighed. 'You know exactly what the company is offering, Roger.'

Although Coast and Country was virtually hers, Bridget always spoke of 'the company' as if it were some entity with a life and will of its own over which she had no control.

Roger eased himself out of his chair and stood up, then: 'Yes, well . . . It seems to be the only way out . . . I agree.'

'You mean that you will accept the company's offer?'

'Yes.'

'Good!'

Wednesday 5 May

Wycliffe was awakened by quarrelling gulls. The curtains of the little window were undrawn and he was looking out at a blue sky with fluffy white clouds. He eased himself out of bed with difficulty but avoided disturbing Helen. Then, in shirt, trousers and slippers, he left the house by the front door.

It was a morning, as somebody once said, 'Fresh from the hand of God.' In the low light most things had a dual existence, in substance and in shadow; the sea alone had definition and wholeness, glittering under the sun. The cottages were silent and blind and Wycliffe was surprised to see a man on the shore, staring out to sea, solitary and enigmatic, like a figure from a Friedrich painting.

Wycliffe crunched over the shingle towards him. 'A beautiful morning.'

The man turned. He was in his middle to late thirties, loose limbed and dark, with unquiet eyes and the taut features of a man at odds with himself. 'Yes, it is a beautiful morning, but if you live in this place most mornings are.'

'You live here – here in the cove?'

The man pointed to one of the cottages. 'That's mine; at least I rent it. I've lived there for more than ten years.' He went on, 'I know who you are. As you can imagine there are not many secrets among the cove community.' He held out a very clean, bony hand. 'My name is Harvey – John Harvey. Come and have a coffee with me.'

Wycliffe looked at his watch; it was half-past six; Helen would not be about for another hour.

John Harvey's cottage was on the east side of the cove, opposite the one where the Wycliffes were staying, and even nearer the sea. In fact it was built out on a rocky promontory and in a south-westerly gale spray, at least, must have been carried over the roof.

Parked at the side of the cottage and, to some extent, sheltered from the sea was a rattle-trap Deux-Chevaux. Harvey said, 'I call him Boanerges because he makes such a hell of a row.'

In the living room most of the wall space was occupied by books though at the bottom of the stairs an area of white wall had been reserved for a framed oil-painting of the cove as seen from the sea. Wycliffe was impressed; the painter had caught that sense of remoteness, both magical and sinister, which he had experienced when he first set eyes on the place.

Harvey said, 'I sometimes think that my books will eventually squeeze me into the roof space; one of the penalties of being a bachelor – most women are great pruners. Anyway, I'll make the coffee while you make yourself at home.'

It was strange, the man's manner was casual, even playful, but Wycliffe suspected an underlying purpose. He was interested and, as always, the books drew him. He glanced over the shelves, searching for some sort of focus, but found none. The fiction content was small and restricted to a few English, French and Russian classics, but the non-fiction ranged through the sciences, philosophy, history and the arts with a fine lack of discrimination. Wycliffe, survivor of that endangered species addicted to self-improvement, wondered if he had stumbled upon a kindred spirit.

Harvey came in from the kitchen with two mugs of coffee. 'So what do you make of my books?'

Wycliffe grinned. 'I gather you've set out to discover the secret of life, the universe, and all that.'

A quick, appreciative laugh. 'I'm working on it, but I don't get far. I guessed a little milk but no sugar. Am I right?'

Already they seemed to be on a footing which is usually only achieved after much longer acquaintance.

Wycliffe sipped his coffee.

Harvey said, 'Why don't we sit down?'

They sat, and Harvey went on, 'Don't you find this life of ours frustrating and more than a bit galling? I mean, it's thrust upon us without a by-your-leave and snatched away again with neither a please nor a thank you. We start with a howl and if we are lucky we go out with no more than a whimper.' He looked at Wycliffe with a quizzical expression that was almost comical. 'Don't you think the gods owe us something more than that?'

Wycliffe was uneasy at having his night thoughts so casually exposed to the light of day. He merely nodded and changed the subject. 'Do you mind if I ask what you do?'

'In the sense that you are a policeman . . . ? I'm a doctor, a GP. I share a practice with a woman partner and we have our surgery in Porthendel.' He smiled. 'I see that I'm going too quickly, presuming on a brief acquaintance, but it's a novelty to have someone to talk to and, as a policeman, you must see the apparent futility of it all, at least as clearly as I do. As the old fairy-tales, myths, faiths and theories, religious and scientific, wear thin, masses of people feel that they are up a creek without a paddle. Is it surprising that they ask themselves, "What the hell?"'

Wycliffe took refuge in gentle irony. 'So you're really looking for a more convincing fairy-tale.'

'Something like that. Aren't you?'

On the face of it, here was a lonely man making the most of a chance to talk to someone other than his partner and his patients, but Wycliffe thought he could detect a more subtle purpose.

'How did you come to settle here?'

'I came here while my elder sister, Julia, was married to Roger Kemp. She was his first wife.' He added after a pause, 'By the way, is it true that you are interested in Kellycoryk and the Kemps?'

'I know hardly anything about them. I've read a little book about the house and its history. They seem an intriguing family.'

Harvey smiled. 'They're certainly that.'

Wycliffe's interest in the man was growing and he wanted to prolong the acquaintance but he had a limited tolerance of psychological striptease, especially before breakfast. On the spur

of the moment he said, 'I don't suppose you would care to join
my wife and me for a meal this evening?'

'I would like that very much. Your wife won't mind? I promise
not to bore her with my chatter.'

'She will be glad to meet you.' He prayed without much confidence that this might be so. Anxious to put it to the test, he
looked at his watch. 'I must be getting back. My wife will think
I'm lost.'

Wycliffe was seen off at the door; a few yards of sparse and
stony turf separated the house from dark rocks splashed with
orange lichen, a shingle beach, and then the sea.

'Thanks for the coffee . . . See you about seven, then.'

Wycliffe crossed the bridge and arrived back at the cottage
to find Helen downstairs in her dressing gown.

'Nice walk?'

'I've just had coffee with a chap called John Harvey, he's a
doctor, and Julia's brother.'

'Who's Julia? Should I know her?'

'Julia was Roger's first wife; her brother lives in a cottage
across the cove.'

'Did you find out what happened to her?'

'No, it only cropped up and I didn't have a chance to ask.'

Helen, in the act of putting coffee into the percolator, turned
to look at him. 'Does he live alone?'

'Apparently . . . I've put my foot in it. I've asked him over
for a meal this evening.'

Helen said nothing.

'Are you annoyed?'

'Not really. I suppose we owe the poor man something if we
are going to pump him about his relatives.'

'We?'

'Well, I can't pretend I'm not curious.'

Isobel, lying in bed, stared at the ceiling and tried to impose a
pattern on the cracks. As a little girl, with Crispin, allowed to
amuse themselves in the library, she had watched her father
doing the same thing, and she had understood. Sometimes she
wondered if, after all, she had more in common with her father
than she was inclined to admit. Perhaps it would have been
possible . . . But it was too late now.

A few minutes ago the old Volvo had chuntered out of the yard; Agnes, on her weekly visit to a supermarket in Truro.

Now Radio 2, subdued to incomprehensibility, just held the silence at bay.

Her father would be in his library and Crispin, if he wasn't at the Northern Garden, would be somewhere in the house, as unobtrusive and remote as a mouse in the woodwork.

She had grown up surrounded by unused or empty rooms in a house which she hated, a house that was no longer a home, buried in a wilderness. At school she had envied the other girls who seemed to lead defined lives in real houses.

She spoke to her ceiling. 'I wish . . .' But she could not even formulate her wish.

There was a tap at the door and, to her surprise, Crispin came in. He looked secretive. 'Agnes has gone to Truro . . .'

'What about it?'

He went to the window and stood, looking out. 'I was thinking about what we talked about the other night and there's something I want to show you.' He added after a moment, 'I think you should see it.'

'See what?'

'It's in the ruins. I don't want us to be over there when Agnes gets back.'

'All right, if I must.' She was wary of upsetting Crispin again.

She got out of bed and in almost the same movement pulled off her nightdress. Crispin made for the door. 'I'll wait for you.'

Isobel caught sight of herself in the glass; she was frowning. What makes me do it to him?

A few minutes later they were in the yard. Through a gap in the boundary wall they entered an area of tussocky grass and scrub where uneven dwarf walls emerged to a height of a foot or two in some forgotten plan. Otherwise there was little to show for the Tudor building which had once been the home of the Kemps. From somewhere away to their left they could hear the stream as it plunged underground. The whole area had been a favourite place to play when they were children.

Crispin led the way through the ruins to a flight of steep granite steps, sixteen of them, leading below ground to a stout, padlocked door which carried a faded warning in red paint,

'Danger! Keep Out'. The steps were maintained to give access to the underground stream.

Isobel said, 'You haven't got a key.'

'I don't need one.' Crispin went to work with a piece of stout wire and in a short time the door was open. Padlock and hinges were well oiled. As they passed through the door the sound of the stream which had increased as they descended the steps now came at them in a subdued rush.

They were in a tunnel, arched over, nine or ten feet wide and of indeterminate length. The water slid smoothly in its stone channel only to be swallowed up in the darkness a few yards ahead. There was a narrow, paved walkway beside the stream, coated with slime, and the air was dank. The lack of headroom forced them to stoop as they walked.

Crispin said, 'Come on, it's in Mayne's Closet. I've got a torch.'

None of this was new to Isobel though childhood visits had been rare and strictly controlled. She followed Crispin along the walkway for twenty yards or so until they reached a narrow opening in the tunnel wall just large enough for an average man to squeeze through.

Scarcely any light from the entrance reached this far and Crispin played his torch through the gap. It opened into a cavity which seemed to have been cut from the rock itself.

'Come on.'

They were standing in a little room about six feet square. Against one wall there was a raised slate slab like a shelf, known in the family as Mayne's Bed, after the sixteenth-century seminary priest who was supposed to have taken refuge there. Now it had more the appearance of an altar, with two brass candlesticks placed one on each side of a plaster cast of the Virgin. Each candlestick held a half-burnt candle. Crispin directed the beam of his torch to an inscription cut into the slate:

> Julia Constance Kemp née Harvey
> died 13 June 1988, aged 37 years.
> Pray for her Soul.

Isobel could scarcely control her astonishment. 'Did you do this?'

Crispin snapped, 'No, of course not! He did.'

'He must come here regularly. How did you find out?'

Crispin turned away without answering but Isobel took the torch from him and continued to examine the surface of the slate. 'It must have taken him ages to cut these letters.' And then, abruptly, 'He's got the date wrong! It was the fourteenth.'

Crispin, as he watched his sister, was becoming increasingly agitated. He took her roughly by the arm and said, 'Let's go!'

Outside Isobel asked, 'Does Agnes know?'

'I've no idea.'

The Wycliffes spent a good day exploring the eastern limb of the bifurcated Roseland peninsula, below Gerrans. They visited the lighthouse at St Anthony, lunched at Place, walked to Percuil, and explored the lush, sheltered creeks on one side, and the exposed cliffs and beaches on the other. They arrived home shortly after five, very tired.

'We've got a couple of hours, so let's start with a shower.'

Helen had never set herself up as a cook; she had a number of simple menus which she could lay on to order; usually they were basic and tasty, but without frills. This one was likely to be more basic than most.

'It's more or less what we would have had anyway. A cold soup, stir-fry chicken with boiled rice and herbs; fresh fruit salad to follow. I hope he likes garlic.'

Wycliffe said, 'I think he wants to talk.'

Harvey arrived shortly after seven, wearing a suit, and Wycliffe thought he noticed a subtle change in him, a certain reserve. Perhaps it went with the suit or it could have been due to a shyness with women. At any rate, with Helen's calculated informality they drank sherry in the kitchen and moved, together with the soup, into the living room. By that time conversation was free and easy.

Inevitably it turned to crime and criminality, to individual responsibility and, of course, to the old chestnut, heredity versus environment. Wycliffe said that was a chicken-and-egg situation while Helen cunningly went on to suggest that families with a well-documented historical lineage must provide a rich source of material for research into inheritance patterns. Wycliffe followed suit with, 'The Kemps, for example.'

By this time they had reached the dessert and were comfortably afloat on Wycliffe's Chablis.

Harvey said, 'Of course my connection with the family is not all that close; my sister married Roger Kemp. At the time I was a schoolboy but later, as a newly fledged GP, when an opening cropped up here it seemed tailor made. At that time the whole cove was in Roger's direct gift and this cottage was available, so here I am.'

'Your sister died?' Helen put the question gently.

'She was drowned in a boating accident five years ago leaving the two children. Isobel was sixteen and Crispin fourteen.'

The Wycliffes murmured genuine expressions of sympathy and Helen said, 'Terrible for the children.'

'Yes, it affected Isobel in particular. It seems to have influenced her development in an unhealthy way. Only recently she told me that she was attending seances in the hope of getting in touch with her mother.

'Anyway, getting back to the subject, what you say about the lineage is quite true. In fact, Roger is supposed to be writing a history of the family. Being Catholics they've kept their line more obviously distinct, and so they're even better grist for the researcher's mill.'

'They dutifully married into Catholic families?'

'Oh, invariably. As Charles will tell you, I'm an apostate.' Harvey grinned. 'Grand old word that! But Julia was a devout adherent and the present Mrs Roger at least goes through the motions.'

After a fair amount of wine Harvey was now on to brandy with his coffee and it was beginning to show in a metaphorical unbuttoning.

'My sister was a very unfortunate girl. She was intelligent – perhaps too intelligent – and talented. She could have done almost anything; she could certainly have made a name for herself as a painter.' He broke off. 'You may have noticed one of her paintings at my place, Charles. But Julia was also one of life's misfits, hypersensitive, only interested in what was beyond her reach, and deeply frustrated.'

Harvey sighed. 'A very unhappy young woman, and difficult to live with.'

He brooded over his coffee, fiddling with the handle of his

cup. 'The atmosphere at Kellycoryk didn't help. It was a strange household; Roger tried, but he was incapable of understanding her . . .' He pushed his cup and saucer away. 'Of course, Clare was there then.'

'Clare?' Wycliffe playing dumb.

'Clare Jordan, who now has the antique shop. She is Roger's cousin and she lost her parents when she was a child. She was brought up at Kellycoryk along with her three cousins . . . Anyway, Roger did his best according to his lights but he was incapable of coping with Julia. Nobody was to blame. It was inevitable.'

Wycliffe risked, 'What was inevitable?'

Harvey looked at him, his brown eyes suddenly wary, then he seemed to make up his mind. 'I know we all pretend that it was an accident, but I am quite sure that Julia committed suicide. I don't believe for one moment that she fell overboard.'

'But the inquest verdict was accidental death?'

'There was no inquest; the body was never recovered.'

Wycliffe was hesitant, wanting to know but not wanting to appear inquisitive. 'But Roger was able to marry again.'

'Yes, he applied to the High Court and was granted leave to presume death.' Harvey smiled. 'Roger would never have thought of such a thing; his future father-in-law organized all that.' A flavour of bitterness?

Harvey drained his coffee cup and Helen refilled it. Wycliffe drew the curtains over the darkened window and for a while they sat in silence. Already the Wycliffes had ceased to hear the constant swish of little waves rippling along the shore.

Wycliffe said, 'It's sad, even for an outsider, to see an historic estate like Kellycoryk sinking into decline; it must be very hard for Kemp.'

Harvey nodded. 'All the harder when there's money in the family. Bridget, his second wife, is a rich woman. But she works hard for it, and if she's unwilling to put her money into the place, being realistic, who can blame her?'

'She is actually in business?'

'Oh, yes. Bridget *is* Coast and Country; she has a staff, of course, but she's the drive behind it.'

'The company that leases the cove?'

'Exactly. Odd, isn't it?'

At shortly after midnight Wycliffe said, 'What about a nightcap?'

'No, thanks; it's been a lovely evening for an old bachelor but I have to work in the morning.' They saw him off, and watched him as he made his way across the cove. There is no such thing as total darkness on the shore.

Later, in bed, Helen said, 'A very interesting man; but that was very odd about his sister.'

Wycliffe yawned. 'There's something going on here but we shan't be around to discover what.'

Chapter Three

On Thursday evenings Bridget had a regular date with the Wilsons in St Mawes to play Scrabble. As usual it was after midnight when she left for the drive home and, as usual, Ann and Gerry came to their gate to see her off.

Gerry said, 'Your night again, Bridgie. But *ziphiiform* – I ask you! Three i's and a z! You wait, young woman; next Thursday the Wilsons will have their revenge if it means swallowing the *Shorter Oxford*, both volumes.'

Bridget laughed; she was on a high. Winning was what life was about. She let in the clutch and the car took to the slope with a screech of tyres. She switched on the radio, an orchestra, muted and treacly, but company.

The road home was narrow, twisted, undulating, and often forked, but she knew every inch. The night was quiet and clear and on the higher ground a half-moon and stars made the car lights superfluous. The little houses she passed were in darkness. Bridget enjoyed the run home at night; she took a pride in her driving skills as in all the other things that she did well.

She was coming to Hendra Croft, a copse and a patch of green verge, less than three miles from home, when her headlights picked out a familiar figure, standing on the verge, holding on to a tree branch, and signalling her to stop. She pulled in, two wheels on the verge.

'Thanks, I was counting on you, I've twisted my ankle and knee and I can't walk very well . . . If I can get into the back I can hold my leg out straight . . .'

Bridget got out of the car. 'Hold on to me . . . Now!'

Bridget prided herself on calm efficiency in all circumstances and it worked. She got back into the driving seat. 'Are

you all right? Try not to move about more than you have to.'
Bridget fastened her seat belt.

Isobel awoke from a sleep which had been troubled by dreams,
and was finally disturbed by the sound of a car in the yard
below: Bridget, of course! Isobel looked at her bedside clock:
the green numerals glowed in the near darkness: 01.17. She was
later than usual. Why couldn't she leave her car in the drive
instead of waking everybody up? Not Bridget! Isobel turned
over and tried to settle once more.

She could not say whether she slept or not but the next thing
she knew she was listening to what seemed to be surreptitious
movements in the yard. Her window was open and she could
hear plainly. There was someone down there; no doubt about
that. To her surprise, her little clock showed 02.31, so she must
have slept. The sounds continued, there were footsteps, and
finally she got out of bed and went to the window.

Isobel's room was at the east end of the house and from her
window she had a full view of the entrance to the yard and of
the open shed where the cars were kept. There was a moon and
though the sky was cloudy there was sufficient light to see that
Bridget's car was not in the shed but parked immediately
beneath her window with the driver's door wide open. As she
watched, she saw her father walk around the car to the driver's
side. His manner was stealthy, he looked about him as though
in fear, then got into the driving seat and closed the door with
scarcely a sound. The engine started, and the car reversed out
of the yard and out of her sight. She heard it come to a halt on
the gravel in front of the house then move off down the drive
and away.

Isobel found herself shivering though the night was mild. She
could not imagine what was happening and she was overcome
by a sense of unease.

At a quarter to four by her little clock she was again disturbed,
this time by sounds from the room below. It was as though
someone had tripped over a chair and was making clumsy efforts
at recovery. The room which adjoined the library was little more
than a corridor, its main furniture a giant settee on which her
father would sometimes spend the night rather than trouble to
undress and go to bed.

He had been doing it more often lately so that she had wondered whether it was a sign of something.

Had she fallen asleep? She thought not, but she couldn't be
sure. She got out of bed and went to the window; Bridget's car
had not been returned to the yard. She waited until her father
had had time to settle in the little room below, then, very quietly,
she let herself out into the corridor and crossed to Bridget's
room. With infinite care she opened the door. There was enough
light to see that the room was empty and that the bed had not
been slept in.

Isobel returned to her own room and lay on the bed staring
at the ceiling now dimly visible in the early morning light.

Friday morning 7 May

It was twenty minutes past eight by the wall clock in the kitchen
and the Kemps were at breakfast. Outside the skies were overcast and a thin rain fell half-heartedly out of low cloud.

There was no conversation. Roger was forcing down the ritual
egg and toast. From time to time he looked up from his plate
as though he would speak but no words came. On the floor by
his chair Coryk had already finished a dish of food and was
lapping away at a saucer of milk. Roger was aware of Isobel
looking at him; she had scarcely touched her bowl of muesli;
her gaze was unnerving and when she met his eyes it was he
who turned away.

Agnes watched them both. Crispin ate his egg, dipping small
portions of toast in the runny yolk. His soft brown eyes gave
nothing away.

Roger felt the pressure building, the intolerable pressure of
silence. Somebody must speak; somebody must make the obvious remark or – or what . . . ? He could not keep it up any
longer. In a weak voice, which sounded unreal, he said, 'Bridget
is late getting back this morning.'

The expression on Isobel's face left him in no doubt.

Agnes was pouring herself a second cup of coffee. 'I don't
think her ladyship has been out this morning. When I came
down Timmy was whining to go out and he's in the yard now.'

Roger cast about for the right response and took refuge in
irritation. He snapped, 'Why didn't you say? It's obvious if the

dog's here, Bridget hasn't been out; she could be unwell.' Even
to him it sounded hollow.

Agnes looked at him. 'What's the matter with you? Tell me
if I'm wrong, but I assumed that she could stay in bed if she
wanted to.'

Roger flushed and mumbled, 'I'd better go up and see what's
happening.'

In Isobel's ears none of the things being said sounded real;
more like a play-reading by poor actors.

Roger let Coryk out for his morning prowl then went up by
what had once been the servants' stairs; they were covered with
linoleum which had worn through in places. His movements
were slow and deliberate; it was essential that he should think
about everything he did and said. He could not guess how much
Agnes knew already but she had always been able to see through
his every subterfuge.

And Isobel . . .

The bedrooms were on either side of a central corridor and
only half of them were in use. Bridget occupied the master bedroom, centrally placed in the front of the house. Only a year
after their marriage he had moved across the corridor to a room
at the back and since then he had tried to wipe from his memory
all that had led to that.

He went through the motions, knocking on Bridget's door,
then waiting before he opened it; a charade, but the only way
he knew of making sure that he had a credible tale to tell.
And that way he might come to believe it himself. He muttered
repeatedly, as if in prayer, 'I must keep my nerve.'

Everything in the room looked as he had last seen it two
nights earlier, the night when he had finally capitulated.

'You mean that you will accept the company's offer?'

'Yes.'

'Good!'

The words, the scene, and the atmosphere were stamped on
his memory.

But now the room was empty; the bed had not been slept in.

Roger paused for a while to think what he was about, then
left, closing the door behind him. He crossed the corridor to his
own room which could hardly have been in greater contrast.
He must be careful to do exactly what he would say that he

had done so that he would make no mistakes. He went to the window and looked down into the yard. There was the accumulation of rubbish which he had come to accept as part of the place and no longer saw, like the outbuildings with their crumbling roofs and walls. If you allowed yourself to see all that, then . . .

By standing with his forehead pressed against the glass and looking to the right, he could see the vehicles in their lean-to shed, the old Volvo, Isobel's white Mini . . . But no Mondeo Estate.

Satisfied that he knew his part, Roger left the room, but in the corridor he realized that there was no way in which he could return to the kitchen and say, 'Her car isn't there,' or 'Her bed hasn't been slept in' – not with Agnes and Isobel watching him.

He went down the main stairs to the front hall and turned into his library, leaving the door ajar so that Crispin would find him. There he sat in his padded chair and leaned back, as if to study his cracks in the ceiling.

He needed a little more time.

With faith, justified in the event, that the weather would clear, the Wycliffes set out early to walk the coast path to Gorran Haven. By the time they reached the Dodman the sun was struggling through a pearly mist, the sea seemed luminescent, and Wycliffe claimed that he could already see Rame Head, twenty-five miles away. Helen said it was mist.

They squatted by the daymark, enjoying the view. Helen said, 'I can't help wondering about Kellycoryk. I've been thinking about what you said last night – that there's something odd going on there.'

Wycliffe, chewing a grass stem and offering free board to some ghastly parasite, seemed to have lost interest. 'It's not our problem anyway.'

They walked to Gorran Haven, had a snack lunch in the village, looked in at the church in Gorran Churchtown, then walked home through a tangle of lanes and field paths. It was still short of three o'clock when they reached Jacob's Head at the top of the slope above their cove. Two police cars were parked on the track leading to the point and a uniformed man lounged, somnolent, against one of them.

Helen said, 'Go on; find out what's happening, and I'll expect you when I see you.'

The policeman recognized Wycliffe and was returned to life. 'I'm on radio watch, sir.' He pointed to the roofless ruin of a little building some distance away. 'DI Reed is just the other side of that, sir.'

Around the corner of the building Wycliffe found a dark-blue Mondeo Estate and a Cliff Rescue Land Rover, parked close. And Tom Reed was there, in conversation with a young man wearing a climbing harness.

'You're quick off the mark, sir.'

Reed was a man of some bulk; his hair, now no more than a fringe to his bald patch, was red; he had a high colour, and arresting blue eyes. It surprised people to discover that he was also a man of perception and delicacy of feeling.

Wycliffe said, 'We're staying at a cottage in the cove.' (A fact of which Reed, in common with the rest of the division, was well aware.) 'I happened to be passing. Anyway, what goes?'

Reed ran a finger around between his collar and his neck. 'As you're staying in the cove you must know something of the Kemps, sir. Well, at nine this morning, Roger Kemp reported that his wife was missing from home. She hadn't returned after spending yesterday evening with friends in St Mawes.' Reed made an expressive grimace. 'If my wife didn't come home one evening I reckon I'd know about it before breakfast next morning. But there! We move in different circles.

'Anyway, nothing to get too excited about if what one hears of the family is true. According to gossip, the lady herself isn't exactly Caesar's wife.'

Reed raised his massive shoulders in an expression of distaste. 'Missing persons are a pain in the neck! It's not even a crime to go missing. I've sometimes thought of having a go myself. Anyway, my chaps went through the motions. They established that Mrs Kemp spent the evening with a family called Wilson in St Mawes, playing Scrabble – a regular date apparently, every Thursday. She left in her car around midnight and according to the Wilsons she was in good health and humour. That, as far as anybody will admit, is the last time she was seen.'

'And the car?'

Wycliffe was looking at the missing woman's car. It was

clumsily parked, sprawled over a little mound close to the ruin. The driver's door was open wide and the keys were in the ignition. It seemed to speak of strong emotion: panic? despair? fright? . . . 'This is definitely her car?'

'Yes, sir. And that's odd too. Some anonymous member of the public phoned the nick early this afternoon to ask whether we had any interest in a blue Estate parked on Jacob's Head. That's how we come to be here.'

'It could have been here since last night?'

Reed was dismissive. 'As far as the majority of Joe Public is concerned it could have been here since last week, or last year, that is if nobody nicked it in the meantime.'

Wycliffe said, 'What do you make of it?'

'I don't, sir. The implication is that the lady drove here with the intention of doing away with herself. It's the place for that kind of thing. As you see, the facilities are laid on, so to speak.'

A short distance from where they were standing, on the western side of the promontory, the ground fell away steeply for a dozen yards or so, a grassy slope stippled with sea pinks, ending abruptly in a sheer drop.

Two men in harnesses were crawling over the slope splayed out like crabs with a depleted set of appendages.

'They're searching for anything which might confirm that she went down that way,' Reed said. 'It's known locally as Simmond's Drop, after a chap who topped himself here donkey's years ago, but others have done it since.'

From where he stood Wycliffe could see the drop in profile; where the grass ended a forty-foot wall of rock plunged vertically into clear water.

Reed said, 'No froth, just a surge, which means the water's deep. It's all tailor-made. You don't even have to jump, all you have to do is to jog pleasantly down a nice grassy slope – admittedly, you couldn't change your mind – and let gravity do the rest. No nasty rocks to cut you up at the bottom either.'

Reed was becoming carried away by his expositions but Wycliffe was an understanding man. 'You think that's what happened to her?'

'No.' Reed sounded confident. 'It seems obvious, but somehow I'm not sold on the idea. That car . . . In my experience suicides are rarely in a state of frenetic excitement. Their behaviour can seem pretty well normal until the last minute. In fact, I think I'd be more ready to put this down as a possible suicide if she'd closed the windows and locked the doors when she left her car.'

Wycliffe agreed. 'Of course there are other possibilities; she may be wandering around in a state of shock.'

'You mean she might have been raped or something?'

'It might account for the way the car was left. Anyway, whatever has happened to her you must get on to Search-and-Rescue for a helicopter and let your chaps loose on the cliffs and adjacent fields between the Cove and Porthendel.'

He added, 'You haven't examined the car at all inside?'

'Haven't had the chance, sir. We only arrived shortly before you. One thing I did notice, the driver's seat is custom built and the controls have been modified; an expensive job. I understand she was very small.'

They worked round the car peering through the open door and through the windows. Nothing unusual. The load space between the back seats and the tail-gate appeared to be empty except for a tartan-patterned rug lying in a crumpled heap on the floor.

Wycliffe said, 'I'd like to see if there's anything under that, but watch yourself. If this is a not very clever attempt at a set-up we don't want to queer our own pitch.'

'I'll bear it in mind, sir.' Reed, very dry.

He contrived to open the tail-gate with a minimum of finger contact and lifted the rug clear uncovering a purse-handbag: lizard skin, small and elegant.

Reed said, 'Funny place to keep a handbag. Anyway, she was no champion of animal rights.' He turned to Wycliffe. 'Do we or don't we?'

'We'll chance what SOCO might say for once but I think you should send for them and for a vehicle recovery wagon. Also, as I said, notify the coastguard and Search-and-Rescue.'

From the look on Reed's face it dawned on Wycliffe that he was taking over the case; he drew back. 'Of course, it's your case, Tom.'

All the same he had something approaching a certainty that the woman had not merely walked out, or committed suicide.

The abandoned car, keys in the ignition, driver's door wide, had a contrived look; it was stagy. And the handbag, left where it was found, seemed to give his misgivings substance.

But the contents of the handbag were not immediately helpful though they might become so: a Clinique compact and lipstick, a comb, a few tissues, a foil pack of six Panadols with four tablets left, driving licence, insurance certificate, and a little case holding three credit cards, a blood-donor card, and several tenners, folded small.

Reed was studying the donor card. 'AB Rhesus negative. That puts her among a small minority for a start.'

A few minutes earlier the cliff road, the promontory, and the broad expanse of the bay with its cliffs, beaches, coves and headlands had been, for Wycliffe, holiday country; now they were rapidly becoming no more than the background to an inquiry.

Wycliffe took an Ordnance map from his pocket and spread it on the bonnet of the car. 'She must have left St Mawes by the A3078 but then it's a question of finding out which route she was in the habit of following after that. It's possible that she was seen. The chances may be slim at that time of night but it's worth looking into, especially if she stopped or was stopped on the road.

'I should watch your step on this one, Tom. If it turns out to be something more than a suicide it's sure to attract a lot of attention. For a start, get a formal statement from the Wilson people. Ask them about her state of mind; not only last evening, but during recent weeks. Have a talk with the husband and take it from there. It's just possible that this might turn into a murder inquiry.'

The cove, when he reached it, looked as peaceful as ever but, unusually, a little group of women gossiped beside the stream. They acknowledged him, but he was conscious of a change in their attitude. Did he imagine it or was he no longer just a visitor, but an intruder, perhaps a threat?

He found Helen seated outside the cottage, reading Trollope. '*The Eustace Diamonds*. I found it in the living-room cupboard along with some other books.' She looked up at him. 'So you're back. To stay, or just passing through?'

'Kemp's wife is missing.'

'I know. Mrs Tightlip told me. Even she couldn't resist passing it on. Is that what it was all about up on the headland?'

'They've found her car up there.'

'Are you going to be involved?'

'Not at the moment, anyway.'

The Kemps had their evening meal in a small room which had at one time been a boudoir for the lady of the house and was now their dining room. In it a few items had been gathered together from the rest of the house, remnants of past times. There was a sideboard, disproportionately large, a half-dozen Victorian balloon-backed dining chairs, and a Regency gate-table. On the walls there were family portraits in heavy gilt frames, so coated with the grime of years that the identity of the sitter as well as the quality of the painting were speculative.

Agnes served lamb stew from a large tureen. Roger sat, staring at the tablecloth, and seemed surprised when Agnes passed him his plate of stew. She said, 'There's bread if you want it.'

Roger picked up his fork and in a low voice he said, 'I suppose you all know they've found Bridget's car up on the headland with her keys in the ignition.'

Isobel looked from her father to her brother. Crispin was staring at his plate and his expression seemed frozen into immobility. He looked ill.

Agnes said, 'Aren't you eating, Crispy?'

The boy started, 'What . . . ? Sorry!'

Agnes looked from one to the other, trying to fathom the minds of each, and for once she decided to say nothing.

They were late having their meal and the room was in near darkness. Roger got up and went over to the light switch. 'Let's have some light, for God's sake.'

Isobel had not touched her food. Abruptly she pushed back her chair, stood up, and left the room.

Roger watched her go. Once or twice Agnes seemed on the point of speaking but each time she thought better of it. Finally, Roger dropped his fork with a clatter and got up from his chair. 'I think I'll . . .' His voice trailed off as he shuffled out of the room with Coryk at his heels. Agnes waited for him to close the door behind him then she began to collect together the dishes,

scraping the plates into a bowl. She looked at Crispin. 'Do you
know what's going on?'

The boy shook his head. A moment later he said. 'I think—'

Agnes finished for him. 'Like your father, you think you'll
find somewhere else to be miserable. I don't blame you, boy.'

Although it was almost dark Crispin followed his usual route
to the Northern Garden until he reached the balustraded bridge;
there he stopped in front of his uncle's house. The night was
mild and the door stood open to the lighted room where Molly,
Francis's girlfriend, sat at the table, eating something with a
fork, and reading.

Crispin had always been attracted to Molly; despite the gap
in their ages he felt more at ease with her than with anyone he
knew. She talked to him in plain language, no holds, no subjects
barred, but she never pressed him to say more than he wanted
to and that was usually very little. He was never quizzed.

She looked up and saw him. 'Oh, it's you! What are you
hanging about out there for?'

He went in. Molly was alone and Crispin was relieved.

'Frankie's gone to see a man about a picture – at least, that's
his story. I expect there will be a few drinks in it somewhere.
Cup of coffee?'

Molly pushed back her plate, took a cigarette from a packet
on the table and lit it.

Crispin pulled out a chair and sat down. For more than a
year he had been a regular visitor at Chylathva, usually when
his uncle was not there. He would sit by the fireplace while
Molly went on with whatever she was doing, listening to her
line of staccato chatter and putting in a word or two if he felt
like it. After a certain time, a quarter of an hour or so, he would
get up and go, though sometimes he would stay to clean out
the hen house or do a little weeding in Molly's kitchen garden
at the back.

One morning he arrived as usual and as there was nobody in
the living room he called out. Molly answered him from the
kitchen. 'I'm in here.'

He found her standing in a galvanized bath, naked, washing
herself.

'We aren't very strong on plumbing, but we manage ...
What's the matter? Haven't you seen a naked woman

before . . . ? Anyway, now you're here you can scrub my back.'

Things had never progressed from there. Normal relations were resumed when Molly put on her clothes.

She looked at him now. 'What's the matter? Bridget not turned up yet? I shouldn't worry; Bridget can take care of herself.'

'They've found her car up on Jacob's. Keys in the ignition.'

It took Molly a moment or two to grasp the implication of the news then, 'They're not thinking she . . . God! There's a turn-up for the book. Who found the car?'

'The police.'

'They surely don't think she committed suicide? No way! That woman liked herself too much for that—' Molly broke off. 'Anyway, here's my lord and master.'

An old banger chuntered to a stop outside and a moment later Francis came in. Francis was a younger version of his brother, but either he had escaped the more extreme version of the Kemp features or they had yet to reach full maturity. He carried a framed picture under his arm which he propped against the wall. 'Morris wants to see what else I've got. He's interested. . . . Hi, Crispy! Any news of Bridget?'

Molly said, 'They've found her car abandoned on Jacob's Head.'

Francis looked unbelieving. 'And Bridget?'

Crispin broke in. 'They don't know where she is.' He went on speaking in little bursts. 'There's something I've got to tell you . . . It's what I came for . . . I must tell somebody.'

Francis reached for a cigarette, lit it, and sat down. 'All right, lad; let's hear what you've got.'

Crispin started to speak in a low voice and haltingly, but he seemed to gather confidence as he went along. 'She went to play Scrabble with the Wilsons last night as usual. They say she didn't come back to the house.'

'Well?'

A momentary hesitation, as though he hadn't quite decided to talk, then, 'She did come back. Something outside woke me, I got out of bed to look and Bridget's car was parked in the alleyway right under my window.'

'Anything else?'

Again there was a delay before the answer came. 'Yes, I saw Father get in and drive away.'

Francis, deeply disturbed, glanced across at Molly and wished that she wasn't there. 'You're not hearing this.' He turned back to Crispin. 'Did you see anybody else?'

'Nobody.'

'Could there have been anyone in the car with him?'

'There could have been but I didn't see anybody . . . What do I do?'

'Have you been questioned by the police?'·

'No.'

'Have you spoken to your father about it?'

Crispin made an emphatic little gesture of negation. 'No . . . No, I couldn't do that.'

'Have you told this to anybody else?'

'No.'

Francis was thoughtful. 'It's up to you, Crispy, but if it was me I'd say nothing and know nothing.'

The three of them sat in total silence, and no sound came through the open door. Outside it was quite dark; inside, the light from a low-voltage bulb over the table attracted moths but failed to reach the corners of the room.

Francis shifted vigorously in his chair. 'I've no idea what happened to Bridget but I wouldn't worry too much about what you say you saw. Your father has always had a knack for turning misfortune into something like calamity. He's never learned to leave ill alone.'

He was watching the boy with an intensity of expression which Molly had never seen before. 'Do you understand what I'm talking about?'

Crispin was subdued. 'I think so – yes.'

'Good! Then all you've got to remember is that your father is not a violent man. He couldn't be if he tried . . . Right?'

Crispin nodded.

Francis got up from his chair, 'Have you got a torch?'

'No, but—'

'I'll run you home in the car but I shan't come in.'

Isobel lay on her bed, staring up at the ceiling in the near darkness, her thoughts in turmoil. She realized that for months she had been playing with a bizarre possibility, a fantasy; now that fantasy seemed to have become real in a different and even more terrible form.

She had been deeply wounded by her mother's death. Without warning, the one person capable of reaching into the depths of her emotions had gone. And it had happened while she herself was away from home on a school trip; she felt betrayed.

'It's your mother, Isobel . . .' It was her English teacher who broke the news. 'You must be brave, dear . . . It happened in a boating accident . . . Of course, you must go home at once . . . Somebody will travel with you . . .'

Neither then nor at any time since had she shed a tear, but there was an emptiness at the centre of her being and a vague, unfocused feeling of resentment. There had been nothing to punctuate her bereavement, no opportunity to say her goodbyes, no funeral at which she could begin to formalize her grief. For five years she had lived with a feeling of helpless negation until, by chance, she made contact with the medium and somehow the idea had occurred to her that her ineffectual, bumbling father might have deliberately contrived her mother's death.

Had she ever accepted that as a real possibility? What would she have answered if she had faced herself with the question 'Do you really believe that your father murdered your mother?' The truth was that she had refused to do any such thing because she knew what the answer must be, and that answer would have deprived her of a scapegoat.

But now . . . What she had seen made anything believable. And Mayne's Closet – how did that fit in?

Saturday morning 8 May

A fine morning; a pearly mist over the sea which would melt away when the sun strengthened. Wycliffe walked on the shore half hoping for another encounter with Harvey but aware of his own ambivalent position if the doctor showed himself. However, the door of the cottage remained closed and the windows blind.

At breakfast he was subdued.

Helen said, 'You want to hang about this morning until you hear from Tom Reed.'

'I must admit—'

'Don't worry.'

He moved restlessly about the little house, living room to kitchen and back again; he stood, staring out of the window at a placid, unresponsive sea. He could hear the helicopter droning along the coast in search of Bridget Kemp's body, and once, with a sudden roar, it passed low overhead. He sat in his wicker chair and read a few paragraphs of Jean Scott's book on Kellycoryk.

All the time he wished that he was back in his office with the right to pick up a telephone and demand to know the state of play in any of the cases on hand. He told himself that it was unreasonable, childish and absurd; but that was poor consolation.

Release came at two-thirty with a call from DI Reed.

'Not much to report on the search, sir; the fly-boys have been out all morning but there's nothing so far.'

'And the car?'

'Forensic are working on it but there are a few pointers: only one person's prints on the steering wheel and those are identical with prints all over the place. Some on the wheel are smeared as though the last person to drive it wore gloves. Of course, that could still have been the woman herself.'

'Anything from the rug or the load space?' Reed always saved the tit-bit (if there was one) until last.

'Yes, they found several hairs – red hairs, stained with traces of blood, adhering to the rug. They're checking the blood against the grouping on her donor card. They also found spots of blood on the floor under the rug and on the headrest of the driver's seat. They also recovered several black and white woollen fibres from the rug which could have come from the little jacket she is supposed to have been wearing.

'It adds up, don't you think, sir?'

Wycliffe had no doubt of it. Injured or dead, Bridget Kemp was carted in the back of her own car to Jacob's Head. He said, 'Obviously we need to know more about that journey which began when she left St Mawes at around midnight and ended on the headland, we don't know when.'

Reed said, 'Anyway we seem to be looking at a suspicious death, almost certainly murder – with no body.' One of Reed's profound sighs came over the line, a sigh which seemed to give expression to a weariness with the world and the ways of men. 'It's time to bring your people in, sir.

'Just one more point. I've got a statement from the Wilsons saying that Bridget has been quite her usual self recently. No crisis; no special worries as far as they could tell. It seems they've known for some time that the marriage is little more than a convention but no particular upset recently.'

After talking to Tom Reed, Wycliffe took time off to put his thoughts in order. It was almost thirty-six hours since Bridget Kemp was last seen and the evidence now pointed strongly to foul play. As Reed said, there were reasonable grounds for getting the show on the road.

He telephoned his deputy, John Scales. 'I've run into trouble, John . . . You've probably seen something of it in the reports.'

The upshot was that a van should be stationed in Porthendel until an Incident Room was established there and that DI Kersey and a DC would travel down at once. Back-up to be provided locally.

Doug Kersey had worked with Wycliffe for more than twenty years, first as a sergeant, later as a DI.

'And Lucy Lane, how's she fixed?'

'Lucy's been preparing papers for the CPS on the Union Street stabbing, but if she's through with that she could join the team. I'll check with her.'

'Well, when she's available . . .'

Wycliffe was beginning to relax, to feel in control of the situation. It was strange, his whole attitude had changed; gone was the air of diffidence which belonged to his off-duty persona and in its place was a certain appearance of authority which went with the job, like a parson's collar.

Helen noticed it and said, 'Holiday's over.'

It was early evening when the message came through that an Incident Van was parked in an open space behind the square and that DI Kersey, DS Lane, and a DC were there, ready for a briefing if that was convenient. Arrangements had been made for their accommodation in the village.

The disappearance of Bridget Kemp had at least taken on the trappings of a real case and it was time for him to behave accordingly; even so, he left his car outside the cottage and set out to walk to the village. He wanted to get his thoughts into some sort of focus. As usual they were vague, and peripheral. He was trying to imagine what it must be like to *be* Roger Kemp, a lineal descendant of four hundred years of Kemps, and heir to the family estate, that decaying house in a wilderness which was Kellycoryk.

He thought how strange it must feel to be living in the same house, using the same rooms, even perhaps the same furniture as your ancestors had done for nearly two hundred years, and then to have next door the ruins of another house in which their ancestors had lived for more than two centuries before that.

If that had been his background, what would his response have been to the threat of dispossession? Resignation? Or a desperate resolve to fend off that moment when the break would come, a determination not to be the last Kemp in Kellycoryk? He was inclined to think that he would fight; not perhaps from courage but from fear, the fear of change.

To which category did Roger belong? And if he was a fighter, how would he fight?

Of course, money would always be the final arbiter and two wives with money of their own had disappeared in suspicious circumstances. Was it possible that this heavy, seemingly mild-mannered man had gone to the limit to preserve what was his?

It was one of those south-coast evenings when the whole of nature seemed to pause, all movement suspended; the sea was glassy, the sky windless, gulls perched on rooftops, starlings spaced themselves like well-drilled soldiers on overhead wires, and ceased their chattering. In the harbour it was the same; moored boats matched their reflections and a solitary old man sat on a bollard and stared at nothing.

Wycliffe made his way up the slope to the village; the square was deserted but although it was far from dark there were lights in the dimness of the pub and in a restaurant where he could see people at the tables.

He found the Incident Van tucked away behind the Old Curiosity Shop in a part of the village he had not yet seen. There was the school with its playground, and a small car-park adjoining. To one side of the car-park was a single storey, newish-looking building with a red-tiled roof. A sign outside read: 'Porthendel Surgery. Dr John Harvey and Dr Enid Scoles.'

The van was in position with a police Land Rover beside it. Doug Kersey's battle-scarred Escort stood next to Lucy Lane's pristine old Viva. A few sightseers had gathered, but when nothing happened they would soon go away and the van with its occupants would become part of the scene.

Quite suddenly he experienced misgivings about picking up the threads again, resuming established intimacies, taking his place once more in the hierarchy – a certain shyness after several weeks away. It was absurd, but it was real.

In the entrance cubicle a technician tinkered with the communications unit. He passed through to the main cubicle. The three were seated round the little table: Kersey, Lucy Lane, and a newcomer to the squad whom Wycliffe scarcely knew, DC Lanyon – Clive Lanyon.

Beaming, self-conscious smiles. 'Good to see you back, sir . . . You look better.' . . . 'Good to be back . . .' The ice was broken, and he sat down. It wasn't going to be too difficult. He took the plunge, sketching in the background and reviewing the facts.

'Bridget Kemp went missing on Thursday night, returning from a visit to friends in St Mawes. The disappearance was reported by her husband on Friday morning and on Friday afternoon her car was found abandoned on Jacob's Head, near here. On the face of it she, like others before her, had thrown herself over the cliff known as Simmond's Drop . . .

'There are reasons against that. The main one is that SOCO have found hairs and bloodstained fibres in the back of her car which strongly suggest that injured, or dead, she was confined there . . .'

The exposition continued for about fifteen minutes and included a succinct account of the people involved and of their relationships. DC Lanyon made the occasional note, Kersey seemed to be asleep, and Lucy Lane merely listened.

When Wycliffe had finished, Kersey, chafing at the constraints which the cubicle imposed on his length, stretched his arms above his head and yawned. He summed up in true Kerseyish style: 'So we've got a suspected murder with no idea where or how it happened, and no body. We're not sure if she went into the water or whether she didn't, and, if she did, whether her body will ever be recovered.'

Wycliffe was used to this. 'All quite true, Doug, and just a few of the questions I want answered.'

Lucy Lane, always one to think before she spoke, asked, 'What's the husband like?'

Wycliffe realized with a slight shock that he couldn't begin to answer the question. He said, 'You'll have to meet him.'

DC Lanyon, like any sensible new boy, said nothing until he was asked to, then he was enigmatic. 'First time round, sir, again there was no body, but there was no suspicion of violence either, not in police circles, anyway. Though others made up for it.'

Wycliffe's knowledge of Lanyon was scanty, derived from official assessments and a couple of interviews: thirty-three, married with a daughter, good record, resourceful and quick thinking. Lanyon spoke slowly, with a slight drawl and in appearance he bore a striking resemblance to the Prince of Wales. Wycliffe wondered if he was cultivating the voice and manner to match.

'What do you mean, by "First time round"?'

'With the first Mrs Kemp, sir. When she had her boating accident I was in uniform – community policing in St Mawes.'

'Are you saying that there was a lot of talk?'

'Just that; there was no evidence to back it up, but everybody knew that the Kemps were on their beam ends and that Mrs Kemp's money would have kept the ship afloat a bit longer. From what you've just said it seemed possible that history might have repeated itself.'

'You were concerned in the original investigation?'

'Such as it was, sir, the ordinary police inquiry into the circumstances surrounding such a death.'

'Were you satisfied with the inquiry?'

'As far as it went, and there was no evidence that would have justified taking it further. There was no inquest because the body was never found.'

Wycliffe considered, and reached a decision. There had been two Mrs Kemps; it was becoming increasingly clear that the second had died by violence, while the first was lost in an accident which at the time had aroused gossip, if not actual suspicion.

He turned back to Lanyon. 'So your job is clear; you pick up where you left off six years ago. There must be something in the files, obviously you start from there but go over the ground until you're in a position to reconstruct all that happened on that day. If you need help, ask for it. Report to Mr Kersey.'

They could hear staccato bursts from the communications unit in the next compartment. It was beginning to feel like home and Wycliffe was getting into his stride.

'Tomorrow is Sunday; you've got a chance to settle in and get to know the terrain, and we shall get down to business on Monday. A WPC from sub-division has been assigned to the case and she will work mainly with you, Lucy. In the first instance I want you to concentrate on the two young people, Isobel and Crispin.'

He turned to Kersey. 'Tom Reed's people are going over the route Bridget took on Thursday night in case she was seen, but I want you in on that and I think we'd better get Fox down.' Fox was the scene of crime officer attached to the squad.

'It seems established that she started that trip alive and driving her car, but ended it injured or dead in the back. Where and when did the change take place? Did she return to the house? Kemp has told Reed that she did not, but we need more than his unsupported assertion.'

Kersey muttered, 'You can say that again, sir.'

'All right, but this is the point, whatever Kemp says, in getting to the headland the car must have passed through the village and at that time of night the place isn't exactly alive with traffic, so there's scope.'

Kersey nodded. 'Point taken. Anything else?'

'Yes, you're going to need extra hands. Let me know the score and I'll arrange it.'

Chapter Four

Sunday was a fallow day. Helen went to church at St Endel and Wycliffe mooned about the cottage and cove. Officially the team was off duty; there is a limit to permissible overtime on a case where murder has not been conclusively established. In the evening they walked on the cliffs and went early to bed.

On Monday morning, an early breakfast.

Helen said, 'So you're definitely back in business.'

'It looks like it. I'm sorry.'

She grinned. 'Liar! Anyway, I expect I shall be able to amuse myself. But don't let it get you down; you're still officially convalescent.'

The atmosphere in the little living room was gloomy; the wind had backed around to the south-west and freshened, ripples on the shore had become waves and the sound of their breaking reached into the cottage as a murmurous background.

The telephone rang and DI Reed's voice boomed, 'It's possible that your body has been found, sir.' (Wycliffe noted that he had acquired ownership.) 'Not far down the coast from where you are. The report comes from a retired coastguard so he should know what he's talking about. Out for his dog-walking morning stroll he spotted the body, trapped between rocks at the foot of a cliff, an inlet known as Grant's Cellar. Of course there's no certainty that it's the Kemp woman but our people have to respond as they would to any report of the kind.

'Apparently land access is difficult so there's a small team, with a doctor, going round by boat from Porthendel. Sergeant Conway is in charge and they should be leaving harbour within the hour. I thought you should know, sir.'

Good old Tom. Always the diplomat. Translated, it meant,

'This one is ours until it turns out to be Bridget Kemp but it's up to you if you want to put your oar in.'

Wycliffe tried the little hotel where Kersey and company were staying but they had already left and he spoke to Kersey at the Incident Van.

'Sub-division have it organized but we'd better be prepared to take over.'

'You're joining the party, sir?'

'If I can make it in time.'

Helen said, 'So you're off already. According to the forecast it's going to be windy so watch out for yourself and wear your waterproofs.'

Wycliffe drove over the cliff road to the village and parked on the quay along with several other vehicles including a patrol car. A small group of spectators created an air of expectancy. The tide was ebbing, almost half-gone, and the surface of the water in the little harbour rose and fell in regular undulations so that Wycliffe wondered what it would be like outside.

'DS Conway, sir.' Wycliffe knew him of old; six foot three, curly fair hair, and a large pink, amiable face. 'We've got a good boat, the *Dorothy*, and a good boatman, a chap called Matty Choak. He and his mate have had experience of this sort of thing—'

Conway was interrupted by the arrival of the doctor, a middle-aged man, an outdoor type, smoothed and weathered like driftwood. He came towards Wycliffe, hand held out. 'Sanders, police surgeon. We met once on a Home Office course. They pick on me for jobs like this because I do a bit of sailing. Evidently it qualifies me for retrieving dead bodies from inaccessible shores at inconvenient hours.' He broke off. 'Is it the Kemp woman?'

'That's what we want to find out.'

The doctor nodded. 'Odd business. Odd family.'

As they pulled away from the quay the church clock at St Endel chimed the half-hour, half-past nine, and the strokes carried fitfully on the breeze. Already spectators were gathering in little groups.

Matty Choak was at the tiller; lean and cadaverous, a man of very few words. He was assisted by a little fat chap, who seemed to wear a permanent grin as though in compensation for his chief's taciturnity.

'Grant's Cellar; is that it?' Matty demanded of the sergeant.

'Just below Kellycoryk Cove.'

This was received with a nod.

In addition the boat party comprised a constable, and two men from the mortuary service who had amongst their gear a light stretcher which folded into a surprisingly small bundle.

The south-west wind created quite a swell and the old launch, broad-breasted and truculent, took it on her port bow, punching into the waves and shedding sheets of water inboard. Wycliffe had a love affair with the sea not shared by his balancing organs and he wondered whether he was going to disgrace himself.

It was not far; within a short time they were off Kellycoryk. The little cove, its grey-brown cottages with lichen-covered roofs looked like a picture postcard. Ahead the low coastline of mainly friable cliffs stretched away into the mist. The three-hundred foot platform of the Nare, no more than a couple of miles away, was a vague blur between sea and sky.

Soon they were nosing into Grant's Cellar and shelter. The Cellar, a shallow cove like an amphitheatre, was backed by shelving cliffs, girdled by gorse in flower. To the west the cove was bounded by a small promontory, a crumbling cliff, with a tumble of ominous looking tide-washed rocks at its foot.

At a signal from Matty the fat man eased back the motor and the *Dorothy* cruised more slowly towards the maze of half-submerged rocks. Two walkers, a man and a girl, watched from the cliff top. As the boat edged closer three or four herring gulls rose screaming and wheeling in the air.

Matty said, 'The bastards have just found her, in a few minutes they'd have been here by the score.'

Wycliffe could see a pale form, apparently stranded in a shallow gully between two rocks now clear of the retreating tide. Even at a distance the red hair was unmistakable.

Another signal, the engine was knocked out and, rising and falling with the surge, they were gliding between the blackened rocks. When it seemed that they must go aground, the fat man put the motor briefly into reverse before knocking it out again so that they came almost to rest within a few yards of the rocky shore. During the approach nobody had spoken a word.

The mortuary men stood up, steadying themselves against the movements of the boat. Matty said, 'I want one of you with me, and bring that stretcher. Take your shoes off; you're going to get more than your feet wet.'

He removed his sea boots and, barefoot, clambered over the side. The surging water reached almost to his waist. 'Hand me the stretcher and grab hold of my arm . . .' The younger of the mortuary men managed it without much difficulty. 'Watch your step, the bottom's uneven and slippery.'

The two men waded ashore then picked their way over or between the slippery rocks to the body and the boat party watched while, with infinite care, the dead woman was lifted on to the stretcher and covered with a plastic sheet. The return journey took longer, and at one point the fat man let in his engine and drew the launch back a yard or two from the shore.

At last the two men reached the boat and the stretcher was eased over the gunnel and laid on the bottom boards of the launch.

Matty said, 'Poor little woman, there was nothing to her.' Then, 'Let's get out of here, boy!' And with the engine in reverse they drew away into clear water. Wycliffe felt redundant.

Dr Sanders looked at Wycliffe, who nodded. An early medical opinion could be important as post-mortem changes are speeded up when a body is transferred from water to air. The plastic sheet was drawn back.

Wycliffe, though familiar with death in many forms, was always moved, perhaps by the awareness of mortality that is in all of us. Bridget Kemp's body (there could be no doubt that it was hers) was still clothed, and the fact had probably contributed to its early recovery. The clothing corresponded with the description given to the police: a black and white hound's-tooth jacket (which was buttoned at the front) and a white skirt which, surprisingly, was still on the body. But there normality ended; there were no shoes, and the tights had been reduced to threadwork while the soles of the feet and palms of the hands were white and thickened. The face, neck and legs had suffered from abrasion as well as from attacks by fish, crustacea and molluscs.

With a following wind the going was easier and Sanders crouched to examine the body, making notes as he worked, and by the time he got to his feet they were off Kellycoryk on the return trip.

'She hasn't been in the water more than two or three days; it's just possible that she died of drowning but I think not. There is significant injury to the base of the skull, in my opinion, aggravated rather than caused by bites. There is too much swelling to decide the nature of the original injury but it could have been the cause of death.'

'A blow?'

'A blow which broke the skin – possibly; but you'll have to wait for the post-mortem. In other words, I can't tell you much, but you probably didn't expect me to.'

Matty snapped, 'Isn't somebody going to cover the poor woman up?'

His only other remark came as they were passing through the heads into the harbour: 'Good thing we got her when we did. Wind's backing an' there's rain and a blow on the way.'

It seemed that half the village must be on the quay to see them come ashore. Wycliffe recognized the innkeeper among them. The body, now decently covered, was carried up the steps and placed in the mortuary van.

Kersey was there. 'So it was her.'

Wycliffe said, 'See that Conway deals with the coroner, arranges for the ID, and gets the body across to Franks for the autopsy.'

'What did Sanders think?'

'That she didn't drown. Where's Lucy Lane?'

'At the van with the WPC from sub-division, waiting to know if this changes her programme.'

'No. Let her break the news officially to the family, then she can carry on with her interviews there. By the way, Fox should arrive soon and I want you to use him in tracing that car journey. I'm going back to the cottage to get out of this wet gear and I'll see you later at the van. What are you grinning at?'

'I was thinking that your break has done you good, sir.'

Two reporters tried to waylay Wycliffe but he referred them to Kersey and drove off along the waterfront.

Sub-division's contribution to the team joined Lucy Lane in the Incident Van; a WPC called Milly Rees. Lucy had worked with her before but that was five years ago when Milly was new to the job. Now she was an old hand.

Lucy said, 'Our brief is to break the news at Kellycoryk then interview Crispin and Isobel, the son and daughter by his first wife.'

In the car Lucy said, 'How's it going then?'

'So so. Nobody's straining themselves to give me a shove up the ladder, but you're in the same boat by the look of it, Sarge.'

'You intend to make a career of it?'

'Five years must mean something. Perhaps I'm waiting for some guy with money to fall for me. You mightn't think so but qualified candidates are thin on the ground. Anyway, I manage with what comes along.'

Lucy listened with mixed feelings. Once she had had no doubts but now, with relatives beginning to treat her like a maiden aunt, and with a growing addiction to hot-water bottles, she sometimes wondered.

She said, 'You haven't changed, Milly.'

And Milly said, 'Snap!'

As they turned into the drive at Kellycoryk a sudden gust of wind brought raindrops splashing on the windscreen and contorted the laurels on either side. By the time they reached the house it was raining hard.

Agnes Kemp opened the door to them. She looked haggard.

'Miss Kemp? I am DS Lane; this is WPC Rees.'

Agnes seemed almost indifferent. 'I heard they've found her.'

'Yes, Mrs Kemp's body has just been recovered from a cove a little way down the coast. Would you prefer to tell your brother before we talk to him?'

'No, he knows already. He's in with his books, as usual . . . This way.'

Milly muttered something as they followed Agnes down a short passage off the hall. Agnes pushed open a door and said, simply, 'The police.'

In the large, dimly lit room, Roger sat at a table littered with papers and books, and in the midst of it a black cat, roused from sleep, turned on them a suspicious green-eyed gaze.

Roger removed his spectacles and looked up at them, blinking. His eyes were vague, as distrustful as the cat's, though less threatening. His cheeks were pale and flabby.

Lucy showed her warrant card. 'This is WPC Rees and I am DS Lane. I gather you've already heard the news.'

Kemp said nothing and Lucy went on, 'Your wife's body was found stranded in the little cove known as Grant's Cellar, just west of here.'

Kemp was apparently unmoved. He seemed to be communing within himself and he muttered, 'Grant's Cellar.' He looked up, as though realizing that some explanation was called for. 'Elias Grant was a notorious smuggler of the seventeen-nineties and that cove is where he used to bring his stuff ashore. In the end he got himself shot in a fracas with the Revenue men.'

Lucy, at a loss, said, 'May we sit down?'

'What? Yes, pull up some chairs. So it's like I thought.'

'What did you think?'

'That my wife killed herself. I said so to the policeman who came here when they found her car.'

Heavy velvet drapes and the book-lined walls absorbed much of the light which came from the windows on this grey day. Leather-bound volumes which were probably never opened crowded the shelves. Undoubtedly some of them were valuable but they were as much a part of Kellycoryk as its bricks and mortar. Books and ledgers, plans and maps, letterbooks and boxes of documents were piled on the floor.

Lucy had an odd feeling that the whole place, and Kemp with it, was caught in a limbo between past and present, without a future. She made an effort to rid herself of a growing sense of malaise.

'Do you know of any reason why your wife might have taken her own life?'

He thought about that. 'No, but why else would she drive to the headland and leave her car like that? In any case her body has been found.' The brown eyes sought the policewoman's as if in an appeal to reason.

Lucy was about to speak but Kemp forestalled her, his manner suddenly querulous. 'I'm not going to identify her; John Harvey can do that; he's a doctor.'

Lucy tried to conceal her distaste. 'I've no doubt that will be acceptable to the coroner. Now, Mr Kemp, I have to tell you that there are features connected with your wife's death which require investigation.' Lucy at her starchiest.

The heavily lidded eyes opened wide. 'Investigation? But surely it's obvious; she killed herself.'

'The post-mortem will tell us more, but there are indications that it may not be so straightforward. You will be kept fully informed but in the meantime we need to talk to those who knew her best; her family, friends, and business associates.'

Kemp was becoming uneasy. 'She had no family apart from me, my sister and my two children.'

'But surely, your brother Francis is a near neighbour?'

'Francis? What has he got to do with it? Bridget had no connection with him . . . None!'

He was gathering together the collection of papers in front of him into what could only have been a meaningless heap, and he disturbed the cat.

Lucy, with instructions not to put on pressure at this stage, was soothing. 'Just one question, then perhaps we could have a word with your sister. I think you told Inspector Reed that you only realized that your wife was missing at breakfast on Friday morning?'

He nodded. 'That's right.' For some reason the question seemed to give him confidence. 'Like many couples these days we do not share a bedroom.' It was as though a child, stumbling through a recitation, had suddenly come upon more familiar lines.

'So you don't think she returned here that night?'

'No, of course not.'

'Well, thank you . . .'

Kemp was already on his feet. He opened the library door and, as he did so, Lucy glimpsed a dark-haired girl – Isobel, presumably – hurrying off down the passage. Her father must have seen her but he gave no sign. He turned to the two policewomen. 'I'll fetch Agnes,' and he followed his daughter towards the back of the house.

They waited in the hall. The black and white tiled floor was patterned with cracks and in need of scrubbing, the oak panelling was coated with the grime of years, but the cantilevered spiral staircase with its wrought-iron balustrade still conveyed something of the elegance which had once belonged to Kellycoryk.

Milly muttered, 'The Munsters at home.'

Kemp was gone long enough to make Lucy think that Agnes had required either briefing or persuading. When she came she was alone and inclined to be aggressive. 'You wanted me?'

'We wanted a word with you and with your nephew and niece.'

'Isobel has just gone out.'

'And Crispin?'

'He's moping in his room, poor lad. Not like him at all; he's usually out there working long before now but he's taken all this to heart.' Her expression had softened in speaking of the boy.

'May we have a word with you first?'

She hesitated. 'All right. You'd better come to my room.'

Agnes's room, a bed-sitter on the ground floor, was sizeable but crowded with furniture like a store. There were good pieces, obviously gathered together from other rooms, and among them a grand piano. ('That was Julia's.') There were shelves of books and a television to show how Agnes spent her free time.

She glanced over her room and seemed to think that some comment was needed. 'I bring things in here to rescue them. At least it's dry, and I keep the room more or less warm.'

She found them seats, and sat down herself. 'So she's dead. I suppose you'll think I'm callous and perhaps I am. I wished her no harm but I'm not going to pretend that I'm heartbroken. You think she killed herself?'

'From what you know of her would you think that likely?'

Agnes hesitated. 'I don't know. We lived in the same house but we had very little to do with each other outside basic housekeeping.'

'Would you say that she was an unhappy woman?'

'I wouldn't say one way or the other. My guess is that she lived that part of her life which mattered to her most away from here altogether.'

'In her business?'

'I suppose so, that and other things. Anyway, she didn't spend time with the family except at meals. When she was home she was mostly in her room.'

Not surprisingly, Agnes was being cautious.

Lucy looked across at the bed; a single, slatted oak, from the twenties. 'Obviously you sleep in this room. Do you mind telling me when you went to bed on Thursday night?'

'Between ten and eleven, as usual. I get up early.'

'Did you hear anything during the night – a car, footsteps, anything?'

'No. One thing I can do is sleep.'

'So Mrs Kemp could have returned here from St Mawes at, say, half-past twelve or later without disturbing you?'

'She could've done, but it doesn't look as though she did, does it?'

Lucy was beginning to respect Agnes. 'Just one other point. My colleagues and I have to talk to all members of the family, including your brother, Francis. Can you put us in the picture there? I mean, I know he lives on the estate but I've no idea where, and I know he's living with somebody, but that's about all.'

Agnes's smile was enigmatic. 'Francis! Yes, well . . . Anyway, you can get to their place through the estate on foot but with a car you have to go to Porthendel then, halfway up the hill to St Endel Churchtown there's a track into the woods that leads to Chylathva where they live – I'll spell it for you.' And she did.

'An odd name. Does it mean anything?'

'In Cornish it means "House of Murder" because there's a story attached to the place about a chap who used to encourage visitors only to chop them up and bury them under the floor. It was Francis who dug up the old yarn and revived the name. God knows why, but that's Francis.'

'Thanks.' Lucy allowed herself a mild joke. 'I'll tell our people to watch out for themselves. Perhaps we could have a word with Crispin now?'

'If you must. As I said, the boy's upset. Anyway, his room is upstairs, turn right, and the last door on your right, just past the back stairs.'

At least Agnes wasn't making difficulties.

They climbed the spiral staircase and walked along a broad corridor. Everywhere there was evidence of neglect, of dust and damp and decay. A narrow, steep staircase on their right led down, presumably to the kitchen area; beyond it there was another door.

Lucy knocked and a voice said, 'What is it?'

They entered the room which was small and cheerless. A single bed, a cupboard, a table and chair, and homemade shelves stacked with books and magazines. What was left of the available wall space was covered by photographs pinned to a cork base.

As they went in the boy got up from the bed. 'I'm sorry; I thought it was my sister.'

'I'm DS Lane and this is WPC Rees.'

Crispin stood up and looked vaguely at the single chair. 'I'm sorry.'

Milly, always equal to such occasions, said, 'Don't worry, boy, I'll sit on the bed beside you.'

Lucy told him of the recovery of his stepmother's body and of the impending post-mortem. He listened with no change of expression in his soft brown eyes, but he said, 'We always called her Bridget.'

'Oh, yes. I understand. Now, there are a few questions we have to ask you . . .'

Crispin waited, apparently unruffled.

Lucy got up from her privileged chair and went to the window which overlooked the alleyway between the east end of the house and the back yard. 'I understand that Bridget often returned late at night. I suppose she kept her car in the yard?'

'In a sort of lean-to shed like the others, yes.'

'Did the sound of the car sometimes wake you?'

'Sometimes – yes.'

'And on the night she disappeared?'

Crispin did not answer. He was seated on the edge of his bed, leaning forward, his hands clasped between his knees. He was very pale. Milly, at his side, watched him with compassion. 'Get it off your chest, boy.'

He turned to look at her, his expression oddly sagacious, so that momentarily their roles seemed to be reversed. He said at last, 'I didn't hear it arrive but I heard it leave.'

'It woke you?'

'Something did, some noise down in the alleyway—'

'What time was it?'

'It was half-past two; I looked at my little clock.'

'Go on.'

'I got out of bed and looked out of the window. The car was

parked with the driver's door wide open but, as I watched, Bridget reached out from the driving seat and pulled the door shut. The engine started and the car was backed away to the front of the house where I couldn't see it any longer but I heard it drive away.'

'You say Bridget reached out to shut the door. It couldn't have been anyone else?'

A small frown. 'Well, it was her car and I thought it was a woman's arm, that's all I can say.'

'Did you form any conclusion or make any guess about what was happening? I mean it must have struck you as unusual for Mrs Kemp to arrive home, then drive off again in the middle of the night?'

The boy considered the question. 'Well, I didn't think about it. Bridget had her own life and very often she didn't tell anybody where she was going or what she was doing.' He added with a faint smile, 'I suppose as a family we are all a bit like that.'

'And when the car was found on the headland, what did you think then?'

'I thought that she must have killed herself.'

'Do you still believe that is what happened?'

'Yes.'

'Did you have any reason to think that she might do such a thing?'

'No, but I didn't know very much about her. I mean she had another life quite separate from her life with us.'

'Did you mention this to your father or to anyone when it was known that your stepmother was missing?'

'I don't think I did. I mean, her car was missing too, so it seemed obvious that she had gone off in it.'

'But surely you must know her better than you say. You've lived in the same house with her for over two years.'

'We had nothing to do with each other.'

A conversation stopper.

Lucy was looking at the photographs pinned to the walls. 'Are these all of Kellycoryk as it used to be?'

'Yes.'

Some of them were so faded as to be almost unrecognizable but there were enough to show that Kellycoryk must at one time have ranked with the finest of the county's gardens. Every photograph was neatly labelled with the location and date, and where there were figures their names were listed.

Milly said, 'Doesn't it make you feel a bit sad to have these around you all the time?'

'No.'

There seemed little more that could be said. Time to report back.

Outside, Milly said, 'Poor boy; he looks like one of the undead in search of a nice unoccupied coffin. And that room! It's more like a cell.'

Lucy said, 'I'm not so sure,' but she did not say what she was unsure about. She spoke to Kersey on the car radio.

Kersey was emphatic. 'Obviously what the boy said is vital. It shows the car was back in Kellycoryk before being driven to the headland. Get him to come in and make a statement, Lucy. Kid gloves.'

When Wycliffe returned to the van he found Kersey with a 1:25000 Ordnance Survey map spread on the table. 'What's this in aid of?'

'I had a call from Tom Reed. His chaps have reports of two sightings on Thursday night which could be interesting. Take a look.'

Kersey's blunt forefinger indicated a junction labelled Tippett's Shop. 'It's about eight miles from St Mawes and less than four from Kellycoryk. A resident says that a dark-blue Estate passed through there between quarter and half-past twelve.'

'Could well have been her. I suppose it's something. You mentioned two sightings ...'

'Yes, and the other is more interesting in a way.' Kersey's finger travelled further along the narrow road for something more than a mile and stopped at a junction with a little patch of green. 'A small copse. It's called Hendra Croft and it seems there's a bit of a lay-by where you can pull off the road. It's less than three miles from the cove.'

'So?'

'A motorist says he saw an Estate car, probably blue, make unknown, parked without lights there at around one o'clock in the morning. Thought nothing much about it – a couple having fun. The car's lights came on just after he'd passed and he thinks the car pulled out behind him but he's not sure of that.'

'What have you done about it?'

'Fox arrived and he's now at Hendra Croft looking for any traces that might have been left in the lay-by. I suppose it's a forlorn hope after all this time but worth a try.'

Isobel drifted into the cottage living room where John Harvey was making a scratch meal from a mug of soup and a chunk of wholemeal bread. She dropped two or three novels on the table. 'I've brought your books back. Is that your lunch?'

'What does it look like?'

She moved over to the bookshelves and stood with her back to him. 'I suppose you've heard?'

'Yes. They want me to identify the body; I think your father must have refused, not that I blame him. Perhaps they didn't ask him. Anyway, did you want something? I've got to go to Truro for the ID, then I've got surgery at three.'

Harvey watched her as she removed a book from the shelves, leafed through the pages, and returned it. He saw a strip of bare back as she reached upwards. She was young and lithe, and supple – appealing, and she knew it. Always playing with fire. Bringing things to the brink then dodging. And always trying to prove herself; where no tension existed Isobel felt driven to create it.

She said, without turning round, 'They're up at the house now, two females, talking to Crispin, I think; that or searching her room. They wanted to talk to me but I escaped.'

'You'll have to face it sooner or later.'

'Do they know how she died?'

'They didn't say, but that's what the post-mortem is for.'

'Do they think Father killed her?'

Harvey was roused. 'For God's sake, Issy!'

'Somebody did.'

'Leave it to the police. Just answer the questions you're asked.'

'Is that what you're going to do? It might be difficult for you.'

He pushed away the remains of his meal and stood up. 'What are you after now?'

She looked him up and down. 'You must be quite a weight on top of a girl, Johnny. I felt sorry for poor Bridget sometimes,

but perhaps you let her go on top? It must have been like grap-
pling with a little red monkey.'

At the door she turned. 'Don't worry; I shan't tell.'

Kersey came in from the communications cubicle with Lucy
Lane's message. 'I told her to bring the boy in to make a formal
statement. If he's telling the truth we've got the car, at two-thirty
in the morning, driving away from Kellycoryk, probably with
a woman at the wheel.'

Wycliffe said, 'So if the two reported sightings on the road
were of Bridget's car, the provisional timetable is, it leaves
St Mawes at around midnight; it's seen at Tippett's Shop, eight
or nine miles from St Mawes, between a quarter- and half-past
twelve, and again at Hendra Croft at about one. Then at two-
thirty it's being driven out of Kellycoryk.'

'By a woman?'

Wycliffe nodded. 'I'm inclined to ask, which woman? Anyway, if all these reports apply, there's a lot of time to be
accounted for.'

By one o'clock, after his sea trip, Wycliffe was feeling hungry
and decided on the pub. He could probably have had lunch at
the cottage but he had worked himself into the feel of things
and he did not fancy being wrapped in cosy domesticity just
yet. Matty Choak had been right about the weather; as Wycliffe
and Kersey left the van the wind was blowing curtains of rain
over the village.

There was the usual lunchtime cluster around the bar and
several of the tables were occupied but they found a table for
two in a corner by the serving hatch.

Already the landlady was treating him like a regular. 'So
you've brought a friend. It's fish today – hake. A very good
fish if it's cooked properly and you'd better make the most
of it before the French and the Spaniards get away with the
lot.'

Kersey said, 'A nice drop of bitter to go with it and I shan't
complain.'

When they were settled and Wycliffe was brooding over hake
snatched from the very jaws of thieving continentals, Kersey
said, 'Why would this woman, driving home alone late at night,

pull off the road and cut her lights? Because she felt ill? To pick somebody up?'

Wycliffe said, 'There's a different question. We know that somewhere along the line she was attacked, and, alive or dead, her body was bundled into the back of her car. Where did it happen? Possibly at Hendra Croft, perhaps at Kellycoryk. But the boy's evidence suggests that she was still alive when the car was driven away from the house.' Wycliffe took a mouthful of fish with a little spinach. 'This is good! Plenty of dill in the sauce.'

Kersey said, 'I don't believe that boy.'

Wycliffe cleared his mouth and took a sip of his lager. 'Neither do I.'

Chapter Five

When they returned to the Incident Van after lunch the SOCO van was parked nearby and DS Fox was waiting for him. Although he had worked with Fox for several years Wycliffe had never achieved the same rapport with him as with other members of the team. Fox was very tall and thin, he had an inherent stoop, and a protuberant nose so that he looked rather like a choosy bird in search of a worm of which he could approve. But within defined limits he was good at his job.

'I was lucky to get there before the heavy rain.' The ground was fairly soft already and there was a certain amount of grass, but there were two identifiable tyre marks where the wheels on the nearside were off the road.'

Fox could not be hurried but his story confirmed the likelihood that Bridget Kemp's car had been parked in a lay-by at Hendra Croft.

'Two wheels were on the soft ground and left impressions of the tyres. I've checked the tracks against the tyres on her car and while there are no absolutely convincing distinguishing features, there's good agreement. Of course it's nearly four days since the car was seen there; if I'd been—'

'Anything else? Footprints? Signs of a struggle?' Wycliffe tried to hurry him.

'There was trampled grass and the imprint of a small high-heeled shoe, probably size three.'

'It's all on record?'

'Of course, sir. I have a cast of the print and all the photographs will be in my report.' Fox on his dignity. 'I've also taken a surface skim which can be examined in the lab just in case there are traces of blood.' Fox was thorough.

Was this, then, the scene of the crime? If so, what had happened later at Kellycoryk?

A small high-heeled shoe. Probably Bridget had worn high-heels to make her seem taller. It was easily checked against the description Reed had put on file. The grass had been trampled. A struggle?

Like Poirot, Wycliffe should have been 'given furiously to think' but furious thought was not in his line. He liked to accumulate images and impressions and to allow them to form patterns in his mind. He remembered passing that copse – wind-battered hawthorn, or was it hazel? He could visualize the Mondeo parked just off the road in the darkness, then caught in the headlights of the approaching car . . .

If then, the copse was the scene of the crime, why had Bridget's car been driven to Kellycoryk instead of direct to the headland?

Good question.

Wycliffe thought the time had come to tackle Kellycoryk himself. He had been putting off that encounter for reasons which he did not fully understand. Lucy Lane had returned there with her WPC and he would join them.

The rain was clearing and the sun, about to break through, edged the sombre clouds with brilliance. The imposing gateposts and the laurels and rhododendrons that threatened to close over the drive reminded him of that first evening when, like a guilty schoolboy, he had drawn back into the shrubbery to watch Bridget Kemp drive by in the blue Estate that was now acquiring notoriety in its own right.

He parked on the weedy gravel close to the front door and his ring was answered by the ubiquitous Agnes. He showed his warrant card.

'I know who you are. We've got two of yours here already.'

Wycliffe was struck by her resemblance to her brother. The heavy Kemp features, tolerable in the males, were an infliction when visited on the females, and it was not surprising if she looked on the world with a jaundiced eye.

'They're up with Isobel. Up the stairs, turn right, and it's the last door on your left.'

It suited him to join the others; he did not want to talk to Kemp at this stage. For the moment it was enough that he had arrived at Kellycoryk, the house which had so intrigued him from the moment he had first caught sight of it. He climbed the staircase from the empty, dimly lit hall, which smelt of mould, to a broad but dingy corridor where paint was peeling from the walls. Desires fulfilled can have a sour taste.

He knocked on the last door to his left. It was open a little and he pushed it wide.

'A word?'

Lucy joined him outside and closed the door behind her.

'We've just got started, sir. She's been avoiding us – always out when she's wanted. No special reason, I think; just bloody-mindedness.'

'I'll stand in for a bit.'

It was an odd little scene in the circumstances; Isobel was seated on her bed, Lucy had been sitting in the only chair, and the uniformed WPC squatted on the floor, feet tucked in, hands clasped about her knees. Leave out the uniform and it could have been almost any three young women gossiping.

'I said I'd stand in and I meant stand.'

Lucy grinned and returned to her chair.

A brief introduction, barely acknowledged, and then Lucy resumed. 'This room and that of your brother are the only bed-rooms with windows that overlook the alleyway between the front of the house and the yard. We have evidence that your stepmother's car returned here on Thursday night, the night she disappeared. Your room is immediately above where it would have come in. Did you hear it?'

She hesitated. 'I almost always hear her come back. Thursday night it was a quarter-past one.'

'Did anything strike you as different from other nights?'

'You could say that. After waking me up she usually makes a mess of getting the car into her space; then you hold your breath until she slams the door. That night I heard her drive in, but the engine was cut at once and there was no door slamming.'

Wycliffe thought, Spiteful, and too talkative anyway. He said, 'This is very important, Miss Kemp—'

'Call me Isobel, that's my name.'

'All right, Isobel. Did you hear her walking away from the car?'

'No. I usually do; she wears high-heels to make her seem taller and they make a noise on the cobbles, but that night

I didn't hear anything and I got out of bed to see what was happening.'

'What did you see?'

'Well, the car was just below my window; she hadn't quite made it into the yard. I could see over the roof of the car that the driver's door was wide open.' She paused before adding, 'I wondered if you got like that playing Scrabble.'

'You thought she was intoxicated?'

'What would you think?'

'You didn't see her?'

'No.'

'Did you see anybody?'

'No. I went back to bed and to sleep.'

'So you didn't hear the car being driven away again?'

'I don't think so; I might have done.'

'Your brother says that from his window he saw the car being driven away and he thought it was a woman's arm that reached out to close the door.'

'There you are then.'

Lucy Lane decided that it was her turn. 'How did you get on with your stepmother?'

'I didn't. I had as little to do with her as possible.'

'Any particular reason or just general incompatibility?'

'Both.'

Wycliffe was taking in details of the room. It was wildly untidy, with clothes littered over the bed and floor. There was a shelf of books above the bed, a mixed bag, ranging from obvious school texts, through Penguin classics to sci-fi and horror. But the most striking feature of the room was its one picture, a portrait in oils, the head-and-shoulders of a young woman. It was obviously a self-portrait. For a moment Wycliffe thought the sitter must be Isobel, then he realized that it was her mother. There was something compelling about the eyes even beyond that of any self-portrait; they were secretive, with-holding more than they revealed.

Lucy Lane was saying, 'Will you tell us the particular reason why you did not get on with your stepmother?'

Isobel glanced at her mother's portrait before replying. 'She set out to take my mother's place.'

'But wasn't that to be expected when she married your father?'

She made an angry movement, was about to speak, then changed her mind.

'You were going to say?'

'Nothing.'

Wycliffe said, 'Is it true that you have recently been trying to get in touch with your mother through a medium?'

'Yes. Is there something wrong with that?'

'No. I merely wondered if anything in particular happened to bring this about?'

'I wanted to find out more about Mother's death . . .' She added, after a pause, 'I was away when it happened; on a school trip.'

Throughout the questioning Isobel had been sitting with her hands tightly clasped in her lap though from time to time she released one hand to sweep back her hair in a movement of either impatience or nervousness.

It was Lucy Lane who asked, 'What gave you the idea of a seance?'

The girl did not answer at once then she seemed to make up her mind. 'I got to know Teresa – a woman in the village who's a professional medium.'

Wycliffe was intrigued by the girl. She was playing a part which she had rehearsed and it was going to be difficult to discover what she was hiding, or why.

Lucy went on, 'And Teresa arranged these seances for you?'

'No, it doesn't work like that. There's a sort of group that meets regularly at Margot Sweet's house and she invited me to come.'

'When you went to these seances did you learn anything which was new to you?'

She hesitated, then stood up. 'I've had enough of this. You don't understand! You are supposed to be trying to find out what happened to Bridget. You are not really interested in my mother.'

Wycliffe intervened. 'But if I say that I am interested in what happened to your mother, would that make a difference? Remember that if there were suspicious circumstances surrounding your mother's death it would be my business to investigate them and your responsibility to help me.'

Her reaction was immediate; the mask slipped to reveal a

frightened girl. 'I'm not saying that there was anything like that . . . I just wanted to know what had happened – that's all. This is something in the family. It is none of your business!'

There was no more to be said and they left her. Outside, in the corridor, Wycliffe asked, 'Which is Bridget's room?'

Lucy went to a door halfway along the corridor and pushed it open. The contrast was dramatic; a bright, airy room, part-bedroom, part-workroom, distinctively feminine yet business-like.

There was a white desk by the window, an ultra-modern computer, and filing cabinet to match. The bedroom furniture was also white: the bed, the alcove which incorporated a dressing table and mirror, the row of sliding doors which concealed a fitted wardrobe. The carpet was ivory, and thick.

'Surprising the difference money can make, don't you think?' Agnes's harsh voice; she was standing in the doorway watching them. 'I knew something must've happened to her; she wouldn't have stayed away from choice, she was too comfortable here.'

Wycliffe picked up a silver-framed photograph from the dressing table. It was the same beautiful, doll-like face he had glimpsed that first evening in the drive.

Agnes said, 'Taken a month or two back; she was always having her photograph taken, a one-woman admiration society.'

Wycliffe said, 'Did she have any men friends?'

'You mean, was there a man? I shouldn't think so. Her only chance would have been with a man who had a thing about dolls.'

Lucy was sliding the doors of the wardrobe backwards and forwards. One section was hung with dresses; another with coats, summer and winter weight; there was a rainwear section, another for skirts and short jackets, and yet another for trousers and casual wear.

Agnes said, 'She had enough to choose from. Of course, she had to have almost everything made specially, she was so small.'

Agnes was aggressive and unpleasant but Wycliffe was beginning to feel a sneaking regard for her; perhaps it was sympathy. But rarely had he come across such an instance of two women speaking of a dead relative with such spite.

He noticed four or five books on a shelf by the bed including a missal, bound in limp leather, edged and lettered in gold. 'She was a practising Roman Catholic?'

Agnes shrugged. 'She went to Mass.'

'Was she much involved with the rest of the family?'

Agnes smiled with her thin lips. 'I'd say she was more like a paying guest who knew exactly what she expected for her money. To think of her taking Julia's place!'

'You were fond of the first Mrs Kemp?'

Agnes hesitated. 'You couldn't be *fond* of Julia but she was a real woman, and she tried to make something of Roger.' A brief pause, then, 'Anyway, if you want me I shall be in the kitchen. There's still work to be done.'

When Agnes had gone Wycliffe turned to Lucy Lane. 'What's your broad impression?'

'Of the family?' Lucy considered. 'They're hardly a family in any real sense; they live in their separate cells, physically and mentally isolated, as far as I can see. Have you talked to Roger?'

'No, I think I'll wait until I have the result of the autopsy. You and Rees had better get busy here. Lock the room when you leave and keep the key.'

It was something of a shock to come out of the gloomy hall at Kellycoryk into bright sunshine. As he drove between the gate-posts he looked across the cove and saw Helen in the little garden of their cottage. It seemed a remote and different life.

He was in a strange mood. He had broken into Kellycoryk ... It occurred to him what an absurd expression that was. But that was how he felt. His attitude to the place was strangely ambivalent and he was still avoiding a confrontation with Roger Kemp. He felt like a boxer circling his opponent but reluctant to make contact. It dawned on him that his problem was uncertainty as to whether Roger really was his opponent or even the central figure in his investigation. In a murder case Wycliffe always started from the premise that the victim, like every other human being, had existed at the centre of a complex web of relationships and that it was in the unravelling of those relationships that an explanation of the killing must be sought. So far the process had only begun.

Which brought him to the brother. Why not take Francis next? A nebulous and enigmatic figure as far as Wycliffe was concerned. Time to bring him into focus. He had already seen the house – Chylathva, that was it! Lucy had told him it meant 'House of Murder'. The young woman he and Helen had seen there must be living with Francis.

The House of Murder . . . Buried deep in Elf Wood. Yes, well . . . He must watch out or he might be pixilated.

A message came through on his car radio asking him to ring Dr Franks. He had reached the waterfront at Porthendel so he pulled off the road on to the quay and phoned from his car.

'Charles? I thought you were recuperating.'

'I am. What have you got for me?'

'I gather there is no problem over identity so we won't go into that. As you must have seen for yourself she's been knocked about a bit—'

'Cause of death?'

'Well, she wasn't drowned. Most of her injuries were incurred post-mortem and are consistent with being buffeted by rocks and attacked by fish and other marine creatures.'

Wycliffe and the pathologist were friends of many years' standing but their encounters were always mildly abrasive. Franks, a socializer, with a fondness for women, brought out a puritanical streak in Wycliffe so that he became defensive.

Franks went on, 'I'd guess she'd been in the water four or five days—'

Wycliffe reiterated. 'Cause of death?'

'Oh, didn't I say? She was shot, Charles.'

'*Shot?*' The very last thing Wycliffe had expected to hear.

'So it seems. At any rate I found a bullet bedded in the cord between the axis and the third cervical. Seriously, she was shot through the back of her neck.'

Wycliffe gathered his wits. 'Would there have been much bleeding?'

'Not a great deal probably. No major vessels were involved. Forensic may be able to tell you something from her clothes – what's left of them. Incidentally, I'm not surprised your man missed it. The tissues around the wound of entry were swollen through immersion and he probably thought she'd had a clout there.'

'What about the bullet?'

'Small calibre, not much penetration; 6.35 or what we call a

.25 Auto, something in that line anyway. Of course you can't take aim with a thing like that; it must have been fired with the muzzle touching, or almost touching the poor woman's neck. But your ballistics people will tell you more about that.'

Wycliffe was shaken though he was not quite sure why. Should the fact of the woman having been shot come as such a surprise? The truth was that he found it difficult to associate firearms with the people who, it seemed, might be involved.

'Is that it, then?'

'That should be enough to keep you busy, old chap; anyway it's all I've got. I'll let you have my report sometime tomorrow.'

Shot! And by what amounted to a toy gun. He could not get used to the idea. Yet he recalled that spattered blood had been found on the headrest of the driver's seat. Somehow, illogically, he felt that this must change his whole view of the case. Perhaps he had formulated in the back of his mind some hazy idea of the psychology of the killer and this did not fit.

He needed time to think, or rather to let his mind lie fallow so that images, recollected phrases, odd incidents would rise to the surface, making connections, patterns which dissolved and reformed. It was his nearest approach to what he regarded as logical thought.

As good a time as any to talk to brother Francis. He drove through the village and up the hill towards St Endel Church-town. He found the track off on his left, turned in, and drove through the wood over ruts and ill-sited boulders for about two hundred yards.

And there was Chylathva seen from the other side: no gate, no fence, just a clearing in the wood; and in the middle, the four-square house, stark, with blind windows and a plank door which stood open. The whole scene straight from the Brothers Grimm.

There was a sign on a post, similar to the one he had seen on the other side of the clearing, but this one read, 'Chylathva. Beware of Snakes in the Grass.' No mention of jackals.

Wycliffe was looking forward to meeting Francis Kemp. There was not a soul in sight; not a sound.

He left the car and walked up to the front door. It stood open into a large, low room, sparsely furnished. Opposite the door there was a granite fireplace with a grate full of grey ash, and beside it, in a rocking chair, the dark-haired girl sat motionless. One hand rested on the arm of the chair, while in the other she held a cigarette from which the smoke rose in a perfect spiral. It was more like a painting than reality; static, an instant caught in time.

He coughed, and the girl looked across at him, unconcerned. 'Haven't I seen you somewhere before?'

He held up his warrant card and introduced himself. 'I came in the hope of talking to Mr Francis Kemp.'

She got up in a vigorous movement that left the chair rocking. Older than he had first thought, up to mid-thirties; a good figure, but her features were losing their youthful moulding and becoming sharp. She wore a skimpy jumper, clinging to her body like an extra skin, and tight trousers. 'He's gone out. When I heard the car I thought he'd come back.'

'Who are you?'

She drew on her cigarette and exhaled slowly, closing her eyes against the smoke. 'I'm Molly Bishop; I live with him. What d'you want him for? Is there news of his sister-in-law?'

'Mrs Kemp's body was found this morning on the shore a little down the coast from here.'

'Drowned?'

'No.'

She stood, her cigarette poised. 'She could have been murdered?'

'We know that she was.'

'Oh, Christ! Do you want to sit down? He shouldn't be long.'

The room might have been a pleasant one: wainscotting, with unrendered granite above, and a timbered ceiling. It was neglected and smoke stained. The furniture was basic; where it was upholstered, stuffing was in evidence. The end wall was almost entirely taken up by a giant canvas, a painting of a bus queue at a request stop. The queue comprised both sexes, all ages, and a fair sample of races. Their expressions were vacant, resigned. The scene was ordinary enough, except that all the figures were naked, and looking at them recalled to Wycliffe's memory those mind-bending pictures of the Holocaust.

'Would you buy that?'

Wycliffe temporized. 'I wouldn't have anywhere to put it.'

'Neither would anybody else, but that's mostly the kind of

thing the bastard paints. Of course, he's a Kemp; they're all dreamers. Frankie's thing is being a great painter. If only he'd settle for being good, he'd make a living, but like the rest of 'em he's pig-obstinate.'

'How long have you been with him?'

'Three years, but I'm a local girl.' She grinned. 'A P'rendel sprat – that's what they call us from the village. I've got a job, some mornings, some evenings, in the village pub and he teaches afternoons twice a week at the college in Falmouth. If it wasn't for that we'd be lucky to eat some weeks. I hounded him out this morning with a few of his smaller pieces to try his luck at a gallery in Truro. He shouldn't be long now but if they haven't shown any interest he'll come back pissed. He says I nag him, but if I didn't . . .'

When she stopped speaking the silence was total.

'Is it you who keeps the chickens?'

Her face lit up. 'Yes, and I've got a little allotment out the back.' She broke off. 'There he is now.'

It was a moment before Wycliffe heard a car engine and a little later an old banger spluttered gratefully to a halt, close to the window. A car door slammed and a man came into the room.

'Ah! The sheriff. I know why you're here.'

Francis Kemp was several years younger than his brother, taller and slimmer, his features were less heavy. But he was still, unmistakably, a Kemp.

'You've found Bridget's body; I heard it on the radio.'

'A radio in a pub.' From Molly.

Francis ignored her. 'You know how she died?'

Molly said, 'They say she was murdered.'

Wycliffe cut in, 'There is evidence that Mrs Kemp was intercepted while driving home from St Mawes on the night she disappeared. She was killed and her body placed in the back of her car. The car was then driven to Kellycoryk where it remained in the yard for more than an hour before being driven on to the headland where the body was disposed of.'

Francis, astride a kitchen chair with his arms resting on the back, listened, apparently incredulous. 'I can't believe this. How exactly did she die?'

'She was shot.'

'Shot?' Francis looked at Wycliffe in amazement.

'That surprises you?'

'Yes, it does. I don't know why but I can imagine Bridget being strangled or bludgeoned – but shot!'

Wycliffe said nothing but he was inclined to agree.

Francis was seemingly reluctant to drop the subject. 'May I ask what sort of gun?'

'A small-calibre pistol. Any reason for your question, Mr Kemp?'

'No, just interest.'

'I see. Did you see much of your sister-in-law, Mr Kemp?'

'As little as possible. She had a low opinion of me; in particular, because I don't pay Roger rent for this place; in general, because she disapproves of those who neither toil nor spin with obsessive enthusiasm. I tried quoting the Gospel at her but Bridget wasn't impressed by the lilies of the field as role models.'

It was hard to see this man as Roger's brother. 'How about the rest of the family? Do you see much of them?'

'Depends what you mean by the family. I drop in at the house a couple of times a week when Madam is from home. Clare pays us a visit when she feels like a bit of slumming.' A wry grin. 'But Clare's all right.' Francis yawned. 'Oh yes, and then there's John Harvey. When I feel in need of a bit of sanity I look John up – usually early in the morning.'

'Were you still living at home when Julia was drowned?'

The question, perhaps the background knowledge which it implied, seemed to surprise Francis. His answer was curt. 'No, I'd already left.'

'But you lived there for a time after your brother married her?'

'I was only nineteen and still at art college when they married.'

'And after you finished at college?'

'I lived at home until Father kicked me out.'

'How old were you then?'

'Twenty-three, twenty-four – something like that. Anyway, it was just after Mother died.'

'And when did you come to live here?'

'When Father died and Roger succeeded to the ball and chain. I must have been about thirty; I'd been bumming around

London for years; Rog took pity on me and let me have this
place.' A quizzical look; 'You seem very interested in me, Mr
Wycliffe.'

'Background, Mr Kemp. Background . . . Have you any idea
how Mrs Kemp's death is likely to affect the estate – or you for
that matter?'

A faint smile. 'Good questions. I should hope it will mean a
nice bit of lolly for poor old Roger, but I've no idea what the
arrangements were between them. After the three years, or whatever it is, that he's been with her, he deserves something.'

'And you?'

'What's good for Roger is good for me.'

'I suppose you are familiar with the place called Hendra
Croft?'

'I should be; I've lived here most of my life. It's a couple of
miles out on the St Mawes road. Why?'

'It seems likely that on her way home Mrs Kemp was flagged
down by someone well known to her and then assaulted.'

'Why do you say well known?'

'Because it is unlikely that a woman driving alone after midnight would stop to pick up a stranger.'

Francis nodded. 'That figures but the whole thing is incompre-
hensible. I mean, to shoot a woman and then drive her home
in the back of her car . . . No man in his right mind would have
done that. It doesn't make sense from any point of view.'

For a moment or two he was thoughtful then, abruptly, 'It
could have been a woman. If a woman wants to work off a
grudge she'll take any damn-fool risk.'

'Francis has a high opinion of women.' From Molly.

Wycliffe said, 'Do you have any particular woman in mind?'

Francis brushed this aside. 'No. Just a general observation on
the sex.'

Wycliffe got back to business. 'I shall ask everyone connected
with the family this question, Mr Kemp, so don't take it amiss.
Where were you at around midnight last Thursday?'

'Tucked up in bed with Molly. I certainly wasn't at Hendra
Croft laying in wait for my sister-in-law.'

It was all very smooth. Wycliffe had never met with such
cheerful insouciance from a witness in a murder inquiry. Time
would tell.

As Wycliffe was leaving Francis said, 'What do you think of my painting?'

Wycliffe tried to say something enigmatic. 'Does the bus ever come?'

Francis frowned. 'Of course the bloody bus never comes. What do you think is the point of the picture?'

It was after four when Wycliffe arrived back at the Incident Van. Kersey was there with Clive Lanyon.

'Lanyon's got a bit of news, sir.'

'You managed to dig out the file?'

Lanyon grinned. 'Archaeology they call it, sir. But there wasn't much in it. Most of what there was, was mine anyway. Nothing to make you think again about the incident.'

'Is that the news?'

'No, sir, not quite. Kemp had his moorings off the Percuil boatyard; they kept an eye on his craft and laid it up in the winter. I was there this afternoon and had a word with Mike Garland who runs it. He let fall something, quite casually, that didn't come out at the time. On the morning of the accident when Mrs Kemp was drowned, Kemp arrived at the yard around eleven. He had with him Clare Jordan, the woman who now runs the antique shop in Porthendel. She's some sort of relative and, at that time, she lived at Kellycoryk and often went out sailing with them.'

'So?'

'The point is, Mrs Kemp wasn't with them. Kemp said she'd had to go to St Mawes and they were picking her up there.'

'Why didn't this come out at the time?'

'Well, sir, when you come to think of it, why should it? I must admit I never thought of questioning Garland and why should he have thought it of any importance? That sort of thing happens.'

'So what's your programme now?'

'I want to begin reconstructing that day by questioning the Kemps about Mrs Kemp's trip to St Mawes. But I don't want to wade in if it's going to upset the inquiries already going on there.'

'Fair enough. Carry on, but put DS Lane in the picture and be guided by her.'

Alone with Kersey, Wycliffe said, 'Interesting. It could mean anything or nothing, but it's somewhere to start.'

Things had been happening in his absence. The village hall had been rented and was being equipped from central stores as a fully fledged Incident Room.

'You can see it from here – the slate roof, next to the school. Ready for us in the morning. And the chief wants you to ring him.'

His master's voice. Wycliffe telephoned.

Bertram Oldroyd had joined the force in the same year as Wycliffe; they came from similar backgrounds and they had much in common, including a firm but compassionate approach to policing.

'So you've managed to find yourself a job, Charles. Tell me about it.'

Wycliffe did his best.

'So this chap has lost two wives in five years. Oscar Wilde had a word for that sort of thing. Neither died from natural causes and both had money in their own right. Seems to me the man must be a jinx, or stupid enough to think he can get away with the same thing twice. A lot of them are.

'Anyway, you've made it your problem, Charles, and I'm not going to ask you if your break has done you any good. I'll just remind you that you've got Kersey down there; he's a good copper, so let him do most of the barking.'

Wycliffe had got what he wanted, a free hand.

He turned back to Kersey who might well have heard what the chief had said. At any rate Kersey was prompted to launch into one of his summings up, which seemed to clarify his own ideas but confuse Wycliffe's.

'Now that Franks has confirmed that the woman was murdered – not that there was ever any real doubt . . .' Kersey paused to light one of his own-rolled cigarettes, then resumed, '. . . We can assume that the scene of crime was Hendra Croft and that her body was transferred to the back of her car and driven to Kellycoryk before being dumped in the sea at Jacob's Head. But why take it to the house? Perhaps his first idea was that it should be found there, but he changed his mind later.'

Wycliffe, in an attempt to be mildly co-operative, said, 'For whatever reason, he must have handled the body twice, and though Franks says there need not have been much blood, there was obviously some, and the killer would have had a problem, working in near darkness, to avoid getting blood on his clothing. Perhaps we should follow that up. Possible suspects – what were they wearing on the night?'

Kersey said, 'Would you like to make a list, sir?'

Wycliffe grinned. 'No, I'll leave the easy bits to you, but remember women are not excluded. The dead woman was a featherweight and, if what the boy said is true, it was a woman's arm that reached out to close the car door.'

'In my opinion,' said Kersey, 'that was to protect his father.'

Chapter Six

After the evening meal Roger sat at his table in the library and tried to work up his most recent notes but he could make nothing of them; they might have been written in Sanskrit. He dropped his ballpoint and sat back, staring at the accumulation of papers. Coryk stirred uneasily. The house was quiet. More than that; as he listened, it seemed to Roger that it had become filled with a positive and hostile silence.

He got up from his chair and crossed to a little bank of switches near the door. He flicked two of them and a couple of rarely used ceiling lights came to life relieving the gloom with their dusty yellow radiance. It was sufficient for Roger's purpose. He stood looking up at a framed oil-painting which hung between two of the bookcases, a three-quarter-length portrait of an Elizabethan Kemp. Resplendent in his black velvet cap (with plume), white ruff, striped jerkin and short black cloak, the gentleman sat with his left arm extended to fondle a sleeping black cat curled up on a table at his side. The most conspicuous feature of the cat was a tail devoid of fur over the terminal inches.

For Roger the picture had become a sort of icon which he had contrived without difficulty to set alongside the holy pictures and statues, the paraphernalia of the church, which had captivated him as a child and remained the source of whatever emotional content his religion possessed.

Usually the picture had a sedative effect, but not tonight. He had convinced himself, against the odds, that he was in the house alone. Normally this would not have troubled him but tonight, for some reason, he could not endure it.

Coryk still curled up on the work table, watched him, sensing his restlessness.

Roger spoke quietly. 'I'm going out.' Surreptitiously, as though in fear of being detained, and followed by the cat, he crept down the passage and into the yard by the side door. It was only as he passed out of the yard, through the archway, that he felt he had made good his escape. At this point Coryk had reached the border of his territory and there he would wait until Roger returned.

It was mild and very still. In the gathering dusk, with no clear purpose except to get away from the house, he followed the stream until he reached Chylathva.

The front door was open and he could see into the lighted living room. Francis was seated at the table eating something with a spoon, and reading. That open door (they closed it only in the coldest weather) seemed to Roger to typify something fundamental in the difference between him and his brother; a difference which, secretly, made him envious.

He hesitated to make his presence known. Standing there, unseen, watching, he felt that he had some power which he would lose as soon as contact was made. He told himself that it was absurd and walked towards the door. Francis heard him and looked up. 'God, it's you! Come to collect the rent?'

There it was; the bantering reception which put him in his place. And yet it was he who made it possible for Francis to live there with his woman.

'Have a seat. How long is it since we've seen you up here . . . ? Must be months.'

Francis was eating some concoction from a large bowl, which seemed to be halfway between a soup and a stew. He cleaned the bowl with a chunk of bread which he stuffed into his mouth. Then, still chewing, he said, 'It's one of Molly's nights at the pub.'

Roger was by no means sure of what if anything he had come to say. He looked around the room and saw the giant canvas propped against the end wall; it would have been hard to miss. He looked at it vaguely, with no shred of comprehension, only puzzlement. But as far as he was concerned that applied to all Francis's work as well as to the man himself.

Francis was watching him. 'Don't you ever feel like that?'

'Like what?'

'Exposed – naked – vulnerable, waiting for something, God knows what.'

Perhaps Francis had not wanted a conversation stopper but he had found one. Roger felt threatened by the kind of intimacy to which he was temperamentally incapable of responding. So the brothers sat looking at each other across the table in silence. For both of them the encounter was difficult; there was no question of an immediate putting of cards on the table; it was more a matter of sounding out attitudes.

Francis made the first move, a conventional expression of sympathy. 'I was sorry to hear about Bridget, Rog . . . So it was murder.'

'She was shot.'

'I know. Wycliffe came to see me.'

Roger was shaken. 'Wycliffe was here? It was a sergeant and a constable who came to see me – both of them women. What did he want?'

'I suppose he was sussing us out.'

Roger was finding it difficult to sit still. 'They asked me if there were any guns in the house.'

'What did you tell them?'

'Obviously I told them there were not, that the only guns we ever had were sporting guns and that they were sold before father died.'

Francis was watching his brother with a sardonic expression. 'Tactical reticence, or a lapse of memory?'

'I don't know what you mean.'

Francis shifted irritably. 'For God's sake, Rog! You're not talking to the cops now. Wycliffe told me that Bridget was shot with a small-calibre pistol.'

For a moment or two Roger seemed paralysed then, incredulous, he said, 'He told you that?'

Francis was unrelenting. 'I was thinking of the one that used to be in that chest in what we used to call the junk room. As though the whole bloody house isn't full of junk. Have you looked to see if it's still there?'

Roger, reluctant, admitted, 'Yes, I did look and it isn't there, but it could have gone at any time in the last thirty years.'

'And I could have won the Turner Prize. Anyway, if the gun's gone, what about the cartridges? There was a little cardboard box with a yellow label.'

'I don't remember any cartridges.'

Francis was unbelieving. 'Your memory must be failing, Rog. You should eat more fish.'

Roger was on tenterhooks. 'But what you're saying would mean that it was somebody who knew about the gun and had access to the house.'

'Well? Who do you think killed her? Dick Turpin?'

Roger smoothed the plastic table-covering with the palm of his hand. 'I can't take much more of this.'

Francis stood up. 'I've got a drop of whisky I keep for special occasions.' He went into the kitchen and came back with a half-bottle, two glasses and a jug of water on a tin tray. 'Help yourself.'

When they were both sipping their drinks Francis said, 'I'm not trying to snatch the mat away, Rog, but if we don't face facts ourselves the police will soon be doing it for us.'

There was an uncomfortable silence and it was left to Francis to break it. 'It seems that Crispin heard Bridget's car return and saw it parked in the alleyway.'

Roger looked like a man under torture. He muttered, 'That's what he told the police.'

'Where were you sleeping that night?'

'I don't know what you mean.'

Francis's patience snapped. 'For God's sake, Roger, did you kill the woman?' He added almost at once, soothing, 'Don't bother to answer that, I know you couldn't kill a rabbit, but whether you like it or not you're sure to be a prime suspect.

'Now, lately, you've been kipping down on the sofa in the side-room; is that what you did on Thursday night?'

Roger nodded.

'Then all this business with Bridget's car went on outside your window. Are you saying you heard and saw nothing of it?'

Roger looked helpless. 'I think I was drunk . . .' A pause, and his voice and manner gathered conviction. 'Yes, I've taken to having a whisky or two last thing, to make me sleep, and that night I overdid it.'

Francis sat back in his chair. 'Ah, well, if that's the way you want it. There's just one more thing. Is Clare in on any of this?'

Roger was sharp. 'Clare? What do you mean? Is she *in* on it?'

Francis shook his head. 'Look, Rog, you're in hock to each other, I know that. Perhaps neither of you is in a position to rock the boat. But you know Clare, and she knows about the pistol. If she sees any advantage in dropping you in the shit she won't stop to ask herself whether she's playing according to the rules.

'All I'm saying is, keep her guessing.'

Roger had put down his glass and was staring at his brother in amazement. 'I don't know what you're talking about!'

Francis remained calm. 'Don't work up a froth, Rog, it's wasted. You've never taken me in.'

Roger got up to go, wishing profoundly that he hadn't come.

Francis saw him off. It was dark. 'I can't run you home, Molly's got the car, but I'll lend you a torch. Mind how you go.'

With the help of the torch Roger found his way back to the archway. As he entered the yard a plaintive miaow came out of the darkness and Coryk rubbed about his legs.

Wycliffe was home early for the evening meal. Helen was in the kitchen. 'I went to Truro this morning and stocked up, then I had lunch at Trelissick. The garden looked so fresh after the rain.'

A shower, then duck à l'orange, by courtesy of M & S. Not bad with a glass or two of nicely chilled Barsac.

'Are you going out? There's a promising play on the box.'

'I think I'll go out. I need a walk.'

At a little after eight he left the cottage and stood for a moment or two, hesitant, before setting out across the bridge and on to the cliff road which led to the village.

He was thinking of the two young Kemps, Isobel and Crispin. Both dark-haired and pale; by some remarkable genetic dispensation they had escaped the heavy features of the Kemps in favour of their mother's fine bone structure and delicate facial muscles. The boy in particular looked fragile – vulnerable.

What sort of time had they given him at school?

Adolescence for both of them must have been blighted in that house of gloom. Isobel had responded with aggression, and

Crispin? Lucy had summed him up as 'an iceberg, seven-tenths submerged.' But icebergs are cold right through. Or are they? Wouldn't there be tremendous pressures in the middle that might raise the temperature? He had no idea; his physics had always been weak.

He could not have said whether he had set out with the intention of calling on Clare Rees but he had arrived outside the shop. There was a light in one of the upstairs windows; he pressed the bell and stood back so that he could be seen. A moment later he caught sight of her looking down at him and shortly after that she was unlocking the shop door.

'I'm sorry to disturb you . . . Superintendent Wycliffe.'

'I know. The comforter dogs. You'd better come upstairs.' She was neither welcoming nor antagonistic.

He followed her through the stockroom behind the shop and upstairs to a room which ran the whole length of the house with a window at each end. The room was well used, the furniture, random in provenance, was worn and functional; make-shift bookshelves were crammed with paperbacks and there was a quality hi-fi and a TV. A coal fire burned in an open grate.

'These evenings turn chilly and I like to be comfortable.' She had been sitting, reading, and her book was open and face down on the arm of her chair, Iris Murdoch's *A Severed Head*.

She waved him to a chair.

As she sat down and composed herself it occurred to him that she was a good-looking woman, who, while making no attempt to disguise her age, made the best of herself. Her dark hair, skilfully cut, showed streaks of grey, her features were regular and strong; a hard woman, perhaps the sort who might well prefer to see life through Murdoch's distorting mirror.

'I can guess why you are here; you want me to tell you what I can about Bridget. I heard at lunchtime that her body had been recovered. A tragedy. Unfortunately, I've had little contact with Bridget recently and I can't say that I knew her very well.'

'I think I should tell you before we go any further that her death was neither suicide nor accident, but murder.'

'Murder! But how? Who would want to—?'

'She was shot with a small-calibre pistol. As to who, that is what we have to discover, and it will help me if you can fill in some background; relationships within and outside the family, not only as they are, but as they have been in the past.'

'But why come to me?'

'Because you are a relative, and I understand that you were brought up at Kellycoryk with the Kemps. At the same time, you are probably not so deeply involved emotionally with the present tragedy as the immediate family.'

It was specious, but she was prepared to go along with it. 'I see; you evidently know my story in outline at least. To put the record straight, I am Roger's second cousin; I was orphaned at the age of six and brought up with Roger, Francis and Agnes by their parents.'

'So that you are almost like a sister to the three Kemps.'

She raised her shoulders slightly but said nothing.

'When did you leave?'

A quick look. 'I left when there was a prospect of Roger marrying again.' A brief pause before she added, 'You might say that I took the opportunity to *escape*.' A faint smile. 'I am not ungrateful for what they did for me but the Kemps are a strange family and life at Kellycoryk was a strange experience. You felt – I was going to say, imprisoned, but that's not the word – cut off, is better – isolated from normality by a whole system of ideas, assumptions, prejudices – call them what you like.' She finished. 'There you have it!'

'Thank you for being frank.' He wasn't sure that she had been, but one step at a time. 'In particular I wanted to ask you about the first Mrs Kemp and the boating accident in which she died.'

This did take her by surprise. 'Is that relevant?'

'I have no idea. It is impossible to say what will prove important and what will not. What I can say is, once it is known that Bridget Kemp was murdered, gossip and guarded press comment will force me to look into the circumstances of the death of her predecessor, whether I wish to or not. But, by the same token, the investigation will carry no imputation of guilt against anyone at all.'

It was smooth, but she was not wholly reassured. She would play for time. She glanced at her watch. 'I usually have a cup of tea at about this time; will you join me . . . ? Do you like Earl Grey?'

'Very much.'

She went into an adjoining room, presumably a kitchen, and Wycliffe could hear her busying herself with cups and saucers. A shrewd woman who would tell him only what she wanted him to know, and that would be edited with skill and finesse.

She was soon back with a prepared tray, hand-painted bone china, rich-tea biscuits, and a prepared response.

'Now, about the accident . . .' She nibbled a biscuit, neat and crumbless. 'It was a tragedy . . . As you must know, I was there; and I shall never forget the feeling of utter helplessness . . . We were out sailing with Roger; he was very keen on sailing at that time. Julia and I were close friends. She fell overboard while sunbathing on the foredeck. She had always refused to wear a lifejacket, and poor Roger was really not skilful enough to manoeuvre the boat and pick her up. It was as simple and tragic as that. Within seconds, sailing down wind, we were hopelessly far away . . .'

'It couldn't have been suicide?'

A pause, then, 'Who can say? It could have been, I suppose. Julia was a charming, highly talented woman, a musician, a painter; she wrote poetry, some of which was published . . . But there was a core of instability; she seemed to suffer from chronic frustration. In some strange way she was never able to take any satisfaction in what she achieved, her sights seemed always to be set on the unattainable.'

Wycliffe brought her back to earth. 'No marital problems?'

A shrewd glance. 'You have been listening to gossip, Mr Wycliffe. It is true that Julia and Roger were incompatible, but if you mean another woman, I very much doubt it.'

'Thank you. That is very clear . . . Yes, most helpful.' Wycliffe gave the impression that he was preparing to get up and go but he had no intention of letting the lady off the hook just yet.

'Just one other matter. Where did you board Mr Kemp's boat that morning?'

She looked startled, but recovered. 'At Percuil boatyard where he kept it.'

'You were still living at Kellycoryk at that time so presumably you drove there with him and Mrs Kemp?'

A momentary hesitation. 'Well, no. In fact, Julia had business in St Mawes that morning and we picked her up there.'

'You mean that Mrs Kemp had left home earlier and driven to St Mawes. Presumably she had her own car?'

'Yes, a little white runabout, I think it was a Mini. Anyway, it was the one Isobel has now.'

She got up from her chair and retrieved a lump of coal which had fallen into the fender.

Wycliffe sat back and waited. 'I'm trying to get the picture. Who else was in the house at that time – presumably the children and Agnes?'

'Normally they would have been but, as it happened, Agnes was staying with a friend in Torquay – she used to go there for a fortnight every year – and Isobel was away on a school trip of some sort – Stratford, I think it was, for the Shakespeare thing.'

'What about Francis? Had he moved out?'

'Oh, yes. Francis was already established in the cottage.'

'So that leaves Crispin.'

'Yes.' For the first time she was getting flustered. 'I really can't see why you are going over all this when it all happened *before* the accident.'

Wycliffe felt that he had gone far enough. 'Yes, of course. So Mr Kemp crossed to St Mawes and picked up his wife. From the pier?'

There was irritation in her expression and her voice. 'In fact, Julia got someone to row her off to join us. The pier is almost always congested in the season.'

'I see. None of this seems to have come out in the inquiry into the accident.'

'But why should it? As I said, it all happened before.'

Wycliffe seemed reassured, but he made one more point. 'Mrs Kemp's car must have been stranded in St Mawes.'

'What . . . ? Oh, yes, I suppose it was. Roger must have made arrangements to have it brought back at some time. I don't remember.' She added, annoyance breaking through once more, 'Does it matter?'

'Probably not; but there is another aspect on which I would like your opinion – Isobel's attitude.'

'Isobel?' She was briefly disconcerted.

'Yes. Isobel came to my attention when my wife bought the china dogs. Isobel was here with you. It was obvious that we had interrupted a discussion, apparently acrimonious, concerning her mother.'

She gave herself time to think. 'How extraordinary! I had no idea that you could have gathered so much. Of course, Isobel was greatly affected by her mother's death. She was only sixteen – a difficult age for most girls.' A longish pause. 'I hardly know what to say. Quite suddenly – in the past few weeks really, and for no apparent reason, Isobel seems to have decided that there was something sinister about her mother's death.'

'Can you suggest anything that has happened recently which might have set her thinking along these lines?'

She did not answer at once, then, 'I know that she has got mixed up with some absurd spiritualist group. I believe it centres around a woman in St Endel Churchtown who claims to have mediumistic powers. The thing is organized by a woman called Margot Sweet, a well-to-do widow. They have meetings – seances I suppose they call them.' She broke off. 'I don't know the details but I have the impression that it is since Isobel became involved with them that she has got this nonsense into her head ... A great pity; she is very intelligent and, fundamentally, a pleasant girl.'

Clare had already said as much as she wished to and she was anxious for him to go, but Wycliffe had other ideas.

'When you left Kellycoryk about three years ago and came here, Isobel must have been eighteen and Crispin, sixteen. You had lived with them throughout their lives, from infancy to adolescence.'

'So?'

'You must have established an intimate relationship of some sort with both of them. I can see that with Isobel, because her mother's death affected her so deeply, her relationships might have suffered, but what about Crispin? Does he still keep in touch?'

Clare frowned. 'Crispin is a very different proposition from his sister. I've never been able to make up my mind about how deeply he felt his mother's death.' She shifted in her chair. 'Anyway, I see very little of him now.'

Wycliffe was already on his feet, and they were making the correct noises preparatory to his leaving, when she broke off abruptly as though a fresh thought had occurred to her. 'You mentioned that Bridget was shot with a small-calibre pistol; has it been found?'

'No. Obviously it is important that we should find it.'

She made a deprecating gesture. 'It's quite silly, but I happened to recall that there *was* a pistol at Kellycoryk. We used to play with it when we were children – until we got caught.'

'Can you tell me about it?'

She hesitated. 'It's a long time ago. We found it in a chest in one of the attics known as the junk room. It was small – more like a toy – but when Uncle Jos caught us with it he was angry. He said it was real and might even kill somebody.'

'Was there any ammunition?'

She shook her head. 'If there was, we never used it. As I said, to us it was only a toy.'

Wycliffe had got more than he could have expected from the visit and he allowed himself to be shepherded out into the darkness. He crossed the square feeling vaguely uneasy and in need of something more than Earl Grey. He went into the bar at the New Inn.

Later he walked home along the coast road; a half-moon emerged fitfully from the clouds; the crumbling cliffs looked pale in its light, and full of shadows.

Helen was still watching her television play.

Wycliffe went up to bed and took his history of Kellycoryk with him. When Helen came up he said, 'It says here that, during the religious troubles under the Tudors, the Kemps hid Cuthbert Mayne, one of the seminary priests, in the tunnel which takes the stream under the old house. Mayne was later hung, drawn and quartered in the Market Place in Launceston but the Kemps weren't implicated.'

'Lucky them.'

Helen had come to bed to go to sleep.

Tuesday morning 11 May

After a restless night Wycliffe was out on the shore before seven. There was a low mist over the sea with no defined horizon; the sea itself was calm but it seemed to breathe, rising and falling in a slow rhythm. Wycliffe had not spoken to John Harvey since their meal together; now his door was shut and his windows were blind. The Deux-Chevaux was in its usual place. Was Harvey avoiding him because of the latest developments at Kellycoryk?

Wycliffe was disappointed; at this stage he would have preferred a chance encounter to a formal visit. He was turning away when Harvey's door opened, and there was the man himself.

'Looking for me? Come on in. I'm late; I was called out last night on an emergency . . . Coffee's ready.'

Not surprisingly Harvey's manner was different, a certain brooding preoccupation. 'I suppose you are directing the inquiry into Bridget's death?'

'Yes, but there is nothing official about this visit. All the same, I was hoping that you might fill me in on some of the background.'

Harvey did not reply at once. He went into the kitchen and returned with two mugs of coffee.

When they were both seated he went on, 'I assume that this is now a murder inquiry?'

'Certainly.'

Harvey sipped his coffee. 'I doubt if I can be of much help. Since Julia died I've had very little to do with Kellycoryk. Isobel comes here; I think she sees me as a link with her mother, but as to the others . . .'

'Francis Kemp?'

Harvey was taken by surprise. 'Well, yes. I'm afraid it's difficult to think of Francis as a Kemp. Anyway, he's like me – and you, for that matter – he gets itchy feet in the early morning and he sometimes ends up here. He's a good wits' sharpener when he's in the mood.'

A brief interval to keep the right tempo, then Wycliffe said, 'You mentioned Isobel just now.'

Harvey showed slight irritation at being pressed. 'Yes, well, she's been making it fairly obvious recently, with little or no justification, that she's not satisfied with the accepted account of her mother's death.'

'You suggested to me the other night the possibility that your sister may have taken her own life. But off the record, I can't ignore the bare possibility of a connection between these two deaths, neither of them natural, occurring in the same family within a period of five years.'

Harvey sat back in his chair. 'Well, I can't accuse you of pulling your punches. I suppose I should be grateful for your confidence but it opens up a bleak prospect.'

'Did your sister have friends or connections in St Mawes?'

'In St Mawes? Yes, she did. There was a woman called Holland – June Holland, who wrote poetry ... Oh, yes, and there's a gallery where she sometimes sold pictures ... There must be others but they don't come to mind at the moment. What's this about?'

'It seems that on the morning of the day she died she drove to St Mawes to keep an appointment and was picked up there by Roger and Clare Jordan who had sailed across from Percuil.'

Harvey frowned. 'Does that mean anything?'

'I've no idea. I'm trying to understand the circumstances.'

Harvey got up to put his empty mug on the table. 'Anyway, tell me what you want to know and I'll see what I can do.'

'You've given me a picture of your sister as a highly talented young woman and, if her portrait is anything to go by, she was a very attractive one. Why did she marry Kemp? It could hardly have been for his money. You see – I am not mincing words.'

Harvey's lips were pursed. 'It certainly wasn't for his money. Of course, Roger's father was alive then but everybody knew they were struggling to hold on to Kellycoryk. In any case, Julia was well off in her own right due to a legacy from an aunt with whom she had been a favourite.'

'So the question remains.'

'I think it must have been a whim – a romantic whim if you like; she was only a girl at the time. After all, Kemp had an essential qualification, he was a Catholic, and the idea of becoming the chatelaine of an historic country house probably had its appeal.' Harvey hesitated before adding, 'And one can't rule out sex; Kemp seems to attract some women sexually, though I'll never understand why.'

'Did you approve?'

Harvey looked at him in surprise. 'Me? I wasn't consulted. I was still a schoolboy and very much the kid brother.'

Wycliffe was content. From his chair he could look through the open door at the cove where the mist was thinning and the sea looked silky; this was the way he liked to conduct an investigation, to listen, letting information flow over him and putting in only the occasional prompt. Unfortunately such situations rarely last long.

'When your sister died, what happened to her money?'

Harvey grimaced. 'In her will she left everything to Kemp.' He broke off and looked at Wycliffe with his first sign of irritation. 'But what is all this? Why are we talking about Julia who's been dead for five years, when it's Bridget who's been murdered?'

Wycliffe gave in with a good grace. 'I did explain, but all right, let's talk about Bridget; another attractive, well-off and youngish woman who, apparently, fell for Roger.'

'That was different. Old Jago, Bridget's father, was alive then and he and his daughter made a good pair.' Harvey shook his head with a tolerant smile.

'Can you enlarge on that?'

A brief hesitation. 'I suppose it can't do anybody any harm now. In my opinion they made up their minds they wanted Kellycoryk. There wasn't a dog's chance of persuading Roger to sell, so they went about it another way. After all, Roger was a widower, house-trained and a Catholic. You might say that it was a reasonable match, but by no stretch of the imagination could you call it a romantic one.'

Wycliffe was incredulous. 'You mean that she married Roger in order to get a foot in the door . . . ? But what was the attraction? Surely, as a business proposition Kellycoryk could be nothing but a liability?'

Harvey looked knowing. 'They saw it as an ideal spot, made for their purpose. Fifty acres of woodland-cum-garden; a hundred and fifty of farmland; a stream, a lake, and an historic house fronting on a sheltered cove.

'They would undertake to restore the house and gardens and regenerate the lake. That would win over the conservationists and, at an appropriate time their plans would emerge: an up-market leisure complex. No Mickey Mouse fun-trap for kids and the mentally retarded, but a haven of rest and recreation for those with enough money to lose sleep over and get neuroses about: a golf course, fly-fishing in the newly stocked stream and lake, discreet water sports based on the cove, perhaps a little rough shooting in the woodland . . . And finally, with a few modifications and additions, fully in keeping, of course, with its historic past, the house would become an hotel.'

Harvey grinned. 'Everybody happy – except Roger, poor old bastard.'

It occurred to Wycliffe that Harvey was more closely acquainted with what was happening at Kellycoryk than he acknowledged.

'If you are right, do you think Roger had any idea that he was being used?'

'To start with, no; but he wasn't long in finding out when it became clear that none of Bridget's money would be available to rescue the place except on her terms.'

They chatted for a while and Wycliffe was on the point of leaving when he was called back. Harvey looked sheepish. 'There's one other thing that you may hear elsewhere but I'd rather you heard it from me.'

Wycliffe waited.

'Bridget and I had what's usually called an affair . . . It didn't last long, there was no commitment on either side. Just plain sex. Anyway, it was over before this happened . . . Now you know.'

'Did you meet here?'

'God, no! We met after hours at the surgery. My partner is tolerant.'

'Who else knows?'

'Isobel; I've no idea how she found out.'

'Would she be likely to tell anyone else?'

'I don't think so. Isobel likes to conserve her capital.'

Wycliffe walked back over the bridge to his own cottage. The mists had cleared and the sea glittered in the sunshine. Three older children from the cove were straggling along the cliff road to the village and the bus that would take them to school in St Austell.

Helen was preparing breakfast and the radio was on for the news; the usual mix of terrorism, famine, street crime, and political chicanery spiced with sex scandals. It put his murdered woman into a horrifying perspective and he felt depressed.

'I suppose you will be tied up all day.'

'It looks like it.'

'I met a very pleasant woman from the village yesterday, a retired schoolteacher, and we thought of going across to Caerhays; the gardens are open and, according to the radio, it's going to be a fine morning with rain this afternoon.'

Roger had given up all pretence of work but he sat at his table which carried its usual load of books and papers. From time to time he stretched out a hand for his ballpoint in a reflex movement but withdrew it again. His head felt physically too small to contain the chaos of images and fears, of ideas and suspicions, along with the futile emotions of anger and remorse which accompanied them. From time to time he let out a sigh or a groan causing Coryk to open a wary eye.

Agnes came in without knocking. She crossed the room to his table and stood looking down at him; her face was drawn and very pale but her deep brown eyes, the Kemp eyes, seemed to burn in her head.

'Well?'

'I don't know what you mean. Why are you looking at me like that?' Roger's voice was tremulous, like that of a child threatened with punishment.

'I want to know.'

'Know what?'

'For God's sake, Roger, be a man for once! What happened that night? You were down there. Did you kill her?'

'Kill her? Of course I didn't kill her. My God, what do you think I—'

'Somebody did; somebody drove her car back here and left it in the alley with her body in it, and somebody drove it away again.' She broke off and looked at him with hard eyes. 'When will you ever face reality, Roger? In trying to save this bloody place you are destroying us all.' She finished as though in exasperation. 'I should have thought once was enough.'

He looked at her with fear in his eyes. 'I don't know what you're talking about.'

'I'm talking about Julia. I don't know what happened five years ago and I don't want to know, but I'm quite sure it wasn't the tale you and Clare served up between you. I'm only surprised that you got away with it at the time but you can be sure that it will all be raked over now.'

Roger sat, staring at her, without a word.

'You've nothing to say to me? You mightn't think so but I'm trying to help you – and all of us.'

She waited but when there was still no response she turned away. 'I don't know which you need most, Roger, a lawyer, a doctor, or the priest.'

Chapter Seven

Tuesday 11 May (continued)

It was the day for taking possession of their new quarters. The village hall was within hailing distance of the van that had housed them until now. They had space, and Central Stores had disgorged the required furniture and equipment; much of it, through chips and cracks, coffee stains and cigarette burns, familiar from past encounters. At least it brought with it the right smell.

Wycliffe had a little office at the front which looked out on the car-park with almost the same view as from the van. Already the paperwork had been transferred from sub-division and he had a neat little pile of reports on his table along with a copy of the *Western Daily*, folded back to display a marked news item.

Body of Missing Woman Recovered

Yesterday morning the body of Mrs Bridget Kemp of Kellycoryk was recovered from a cove known as Grant's Cellar in Veryan Bay. Mrs Kemp failed to return home from a visit to friends in St Mawes on Thursday evening and her abandoned car was found on Jacob's Head near her home the following day. The circumstances of her disappearance and death are being investigated and an inquest will be held.

Mrs Kemp leaves a husband, a
stepson and stepdaughter.

This is the second time in five years
that tragedy has visited the family.
In June 1988, Mrs Julia Kemp
was drowned in a boating accident
while sailing with her husband off
Falmouth.

Wycliffe passed the paper to Kersey. 'Sting in the tail there. They
don't even mention the presence of Clare Jordan. If they're doing
that now what will it be when they know she was murdered?'

And soon they would know, for there was to be a press
briefing at half-past ten.

He leafed through the reports. Franks, the least verbose of
men, had contrived to spread his findings over several pages of
typescript for the benefit of the coroner and the lawyers. The
core was, of course, that Bridget Kemp had died as a result of
being shot, at near-contact range, in the back of the neck, with
a small-calibre pistol.

A report from Ballistics confirmed and enlarged on this: the
bullet removed from the dead woman's neck was a 6.35mm,
what the British call a .25 Auto and, in the opinion of the
experts, it had been fired from a 'Baby Browning' type, pocket
self-loading pistol.

Wycliffe was reflective. 'If I was in the back of a car the last
thing I would think of doing would be to shoot the driver —
unless, of course, the car was stationary.'

Kersey, caught in the toils of impending self-denial, was grop-
ing in the bottom of his tobacco pouch for a few shreds of shag to
roll his last cigarette. Accepting failure, he said, 'I've been thinking on those lines and I've worked out a possible scenario: Bridget,
on her way home, is flagged down by someone she knows, waiting
in the lay-by at Hendra Croft. Instead of going around the car to
get in beside her, her passenger gets in the back and before she can
pull away she gets it in the back of her neck, spattering blood on
the headrest. The guy then gets out, removes her body from the
driving seat, stows it in the load space, and drives off.'

Wycliffe finished for him. 'To Kellycoryk where he leaves the
car for more than an hour before driving to Jacob's Head and

finally disposing of the body.' A profound sigh. 'I find your bit more credible than mine, but I suppose they have to be fitted together. A couple of points: you don't account for Bridget getting out of the car and leaving her footprints in the mud; you've also assumed that her attacker was a man, but if young Crispin is to be relied upon, the car was driven away from Kellycoryk by a woman.'

'Yes, and you know my opinion about that.' Kersey had scraped together a few tobacco shreds and contrived to roll a thin spill which he now lit as though performing some sacred rite.

Wycliffe was still turning over the reports in the hope of discovering something that he did not already know.

The team met for a briefing. Wycliffe told Lanyon to follow up Julia Kemp's appointment at St Mawes on the morning of the day she died. 'I know it's five years ago but if she had regular contacts in St Mawes, people will remember her. Her white Mini might help. Talk to Clare Jordan and see what else you can dig up.'

Lucy Lane was downbeat regarding the second Mrs Kemp. 'The woman must have been almost pathologically circumspect. All her computer discs are protected; there isn't a scrap of writing anywhere. In fact, there's nothing much of anything except her clothes and her photographs to tell you about the women. I think we should get DS Shaw down to work on the discs; for all I've found she could have been a couturier's dummy.' Lucy being acid. She went on, 'I've got together a few details of her company: Coast and Country have their offices in St Mary's Street, Truro, and the manager is called Curtis – Ian Curtis. Her solicitor, business and personal, is Ralph Beasley, of Beasley and Fiske, an old friend of her father's.'

Wycliffe said, 'I'm surprised they haven't been in touch.'

DS Fox handed in his report on the investigations at Hendra Croft. Like all Fox's reports it could have been framed and preserved for posterity, but it confirmed that the heelprints at the scene resembled those made by shoes in the dead woman's possession. The shoes she was actually wearing at the time were not recovered with the body.

Kersey's little firework had burned itself out and he had discarded the pitiful remnant to save his lips. He said, trying to look involved, 'So we now know the scene of the crime and the nature of the weapon used to commit it.'

Wycliffe told of the pistol which had been a plaything for the juvenile Kemps. 'Obviously we must search for the gun, starting from there. Let's hope the killer doesn't have another use for it. I'm seeing Kemp this morning with Lucy and I'll set that ball rolling.

'What we need now is to go over every bit of the route from Hendra Croft, through Porthendel and on to the cove. I want everybody who lives along that route and anybody who was driving or walking along it after, say, ten on Thursday night, to be found and questioned. Remember, it's not only sightings of the blue Mondeo Estate that we're after. If the killer was waiting for Bridget Kemp at Hendra Croft, he or she must have got there somehow – most probably on foot.

'Sub-division will provide assistance if necessary and Mr Kersey will be in charge. All reports and queries to him.'

The telephone rang. 'Ralph Beasley, the dead woman's solicitor, sir.'

Thought waves?

The voice was quiet and cultured. 'Mr Wycliffe . . . ? Ralph Beasley. I act for Coast and Country and for Bridget Kemp. I returned from abroad last evening in response to an urgent message from the office . . . There are things I would like to discuss with you . . . Perhaps we might meet? For several reasons it would be helpful if we could meet in the firm's offices in St Mary's Street . . . Thank you; that will suit me very well. This afternoon, then.'

By half-past ten there was a gathering of the press and TV. The Incident Room had come just in time, otherwise the cameras would have had him posturing in the car-park.

It was obvious that the news had leaked out. From the start it was clear that they wanted answers to questions rather than a statement.

'The post-mortem and a ballistics report show that Mrs Bridget Kemp was shot in the back of the neck with a small-calibre self-loading pistol.'

'Have you any idea where the crime took place?'

'There is evidence to suggest that she was shot from behind

whilst sitting in the driving seat of her car when the car was parked beside the road at Hendra Croft.'

'So the killer was in the back and was, presumably, known to her.'

'That is speculation.'

'Has the weapon been recovered?'

'No. We are looking for a self-loading pistol of small calibre.'

'Is it the case that Mrs Kemp's car returned briefly to Kellycoryk before being driven to Jacob's Head where it was abandoned?'

'I am not prepared to comment on that question at this stage.'

Soon the questioning shifted, as he knew it would, to the first Mrs Kemp.

A wizened little man who worked for an agency started the ball rolling. 'So we know how, if not why, or who by, Mrs Bridget Kemp was killed, but are we any wiser about her predecessor, Mrs Julia Kemp?'

'I can only refer you to the news reports at the time.'

A woman reporter tried her hand. 'Are the police re-opening their investigation into the death of the first Mrs Kemp?'

'I am not aware that there was any police investigation. The coroner's officer made the usual inquiries and was satisfied that a tragic accident had occurred.'

And that was that. Not too bad, but there would be other days.

Coffee, and Wycliffe was on his way to Kellycoryk with Lucy Lane and WPC Rees, but this time it was to interview Roger Kemp. For reasons that were not clear to him he had put off this encounter until he could do so no longer. He had in his mind the memory of a sad figure, alone, except for his cat, hands in pockets, watching the ducks feed on the once ornamental pond now being choked out of existence by invading rushes.

They had to ring several times before the door was answered by a young woman who said she was the daily help. 'She's gone into Truro to do the shopping; he's in the library. I dunno where Isobel and Crispin are.'

They made for the library unescorted. Wycliffe tapped at the door then opened it. Roger was seated at his work table and at first sight Wycliffe thought he was asleep, then he saw that his eyes were wide open. He was lying back in his chair, staring up at the ceiling.

It was a moment or two before he became aware of them, then he sat bolt upright and faced them with vacant eyes. He was unshaven and looked like a man who had not slept for nights.

Wycliffe went through the routine introduction and it was received with dawning recognition and a tired gesture which could be interpreted as both an acknowledgement and an invitation to sit down.

Milly Rees found chairs for them. It seemed impossible to establish meaningful contact and Wycliffe found himself making a bald statement of fact. 'I think you already know that your wife did not take her own life, Mr Kemp, and that the pathologist's report makes it clear that she was shot.'

Roger reached out to stroke his cat as though the contact provided reassurance. He still said nothing.

Wycliffe ploughed on. 'As far as you know are there any firearms in this house, Mr Kemp?'

This prompted a definite, almost an emphatic response. 'No! In my father's time there were sporting guns, but they were sold off years ago. At no time since have we had guns of any sort in the house.'

Wycliffe persisted. 'I have in mind a small self-loading pistol which you and others sometimes played with when you were children.'

Roger's eyes widened and he shifted uncomfortably in his chair. 'That was a very long time ago.'

'But you remember it?'

'I suppose so, but—'

'Will you describe the gun as far as you are able?'

Roger spoke in a low voice, scarcely audible. 'It was a little pistol. We thought it was a toy until father found us with it . . . It had a butt that was made of bone or ivory . . .' His voice trailed off.

Wycliffe said, 'I believe it was kept in a chest in one of the attics along with a lot of other things. Have you looked to see if it is still there?'

After each question there was a long interval before an answer came and during that time Roger's gaze shifted about the room and his hands were rarely still. 'Yes, I have to admit that I've looked and it isn't there. It must have gone a long time ago.'

'Where would it have gone?'

A slow shrug as though the question was unreasonable.

'We need to search for that pistol, Mr Kemp.'

Wycliffe felt that the time had come to change the subject. 'We have evidence that the crime was committed at Hendra Croft, that your wife was flagged down on her way back from St Mawes and attacked. The car was then driven here and remained in the yard for an hour and a half before being driven to Jacob's Head, where her body was disposed of.'

Kemp made no move to confirm or contest this version of events. Wycliffe gave him time but all that came was, 'I don't understand it.'

The light was fading by the minute and it looked as though the promised rain was arriving early. The walls of the room with their shelves of books receded into the gloom and what light there was seemed to fall upon Roger's large, pale face.

Wycliffe said, 'You can offer no explanation of why your wife's car was returned here, where it remained for some time, before being driven off to the headland?'

When it seemed that Kemp would not answer, he murmured, 'No.'

'Where do you sleep, Mr Kemp?'

'Sleep?' The question seemed to startle him. 'My bedroom is in the back of the house, overlooking the yard.'

'And you heard nothing of the arrival of your wife's car nor of its later departure?'

'Nothing.'

By that tacit understanding which seemed to exist between them, Lucy realized that it was her turn. She said, 'Your wife ran a very successful business, Mr Kemp, and it is common knowledge that you have difficulty in maintaining the estate. Were there quarrels over money?'

Again there was an interval before he answered. 'No. There were no quarrels. There were discussions.'

Wycliffe intervened. 'It is said that Mrs Kemp was prepared to make a very significant contribution to restoring the property, but only as part of a Coast and Country leisure project. Is that so?'

'Yes.'

'But you refused to agree to this?'

Kemp brought his large, soft hands together on the table top and spoke in a tired voice. 'No, I did not refuse. It was not what I would have wanted but I came to the conclusion that it was the only possible way in which Kellycoryk could survive. I came to a provisional arrangement with my wife and it was intended that we should enter into a formal agreement.'

'When was this agreed between you?'

'On Tuesday evening.'

'Two days before she disappeared.'

'Yes.'

'Did anyone else – *does* anyone else know of the arrangement?'

Roger raised his shoulders in a dismissive shrug. 'I suppose Bridget might have discussed it with her associates and I mentioned it to my family.'

'How is your wife's death likely to affect the proposal?'

'I have no idea.'

'Do you know the contents of your wife's will – assuming that she made one?'

'No; it was something that we never discussed. You will have to talk to her solicitor.'

'I am doing so, this afternoon.'

Kemp spread his hands in a small gesture as though this disposed of the matter.

'Presumably you have made a will?'

'No.'

'Are you under any constraints in dealing with the property, such as entail or conditions laid down in your father's will?'

Roger frowned, and it was a moment or two before he answered. 'If I were to sell the property, my brother, my sister and my cousin, Clare, would each receive one-sixth of the proceeds of the sale.'

'So you would get half. Will that be the situation if your agreement with Coast and Country Leisure goes through?'

Roger shifted uneasily. 'No. The agreement would involve leasing, not selling the property so the provision would not apply.'

Another two or three minutes and Wycliffe was satisfied that he had got all that he was likely to for the moment.

Outside, Lucy wanted to know what he thought of the interview. 'The business of the will and the leasing of the property is interesting.'

'And the rest?'

Wycliffe was casual. 'All of them seem to have reason to lie, or think they have, so you pays your money and you takes your choice.'

'You didn't refer to his first wife.'

'No, I thought we would see how Lanyon gets on first . . . You and Rees had better start trying to trace that pistol, though I doubt if you'll get very far. I only hope that whoever has it hasn't thought of a further use for it. Will you be at the pub for lunch?'

Tuesday afternoon 11 May

When Wycliffe set out for Truro the rain had stopped and a thin mist allowed hazy sunshine to filter through. The roads in this part of Cornwall were made originally for passage between farms and hamlets; they stagger across the countryside with abrupt and bewildering changes of direction, but the names of the places they link together are compensation in themselves: Great Polgrain, Goviley Major, Tippett's Shop, Paradise Cottage and Bessybeneath . . .

Wycliffe arrived at the river and made a slow but majestic crossing by the chain ferry. He was greeted in the city by the cathedral and town clocks chiming a quarter-past two out of sync. Reluctant to play musical chairs in search of a parking space, he asserted his privilege and found a space in the yard of the police station.

Truro is one of those country towns where the old ways have not yet been entirely squeezed out by greedy supermarkets and rapacious developers. There are still substantial businesses which have remained in the same family for generations, and there are doors off side streets which lead to mysterious offices above shops.

The offices of Coast and Country were above a jeweller's, reached by way of a glossy black door reminiscent of 10

Downing Street, and carpeted stairs. At the top, on a sort of landing, a blonde sat at a desk and asked, with no interest at all, 'Can I help you?' That question which has become almost a provocation.

Before he could reply, a youngish Uriah Heep packaged in bulging pinstripes came out of one of the doors, hand outstretched. 'Chief Superintendent Wycliffe . . . Ian Curtis . . . Good of you to come . . . This way if you please . . .'

From a chair, next to the inevitable upholstered swivel, another man stood up and Curtis said, 'I think you spoke to Mr Beasley on the telephone – Mr Ralph Beasley, Chief Superintendent Wycliffe.'

Beasley was an older man, lean and bony, with white hair and a little white moustache over teeth, yellowing and irregular, but his own.

'So Bridget is dead, Mr Wycliffe.'

'I'm afraid so, and, if you have not heard already I must tell you that she was murdered.'

'Murdered!'

Wycliffe recounted the circumstances and Beasley appeared deeply distressed.

'I should explain that I have known Bridget from the very day of her birth and I was closely involved with her father both as a business associate and a friend. You might say that Bridget inherited me in both capacities.' A dry chuckle, instantly suppressed. 'Technically, I am a co-director with Bridget, and the firm's solicitor, but I should add that my holding in the company is a nominal one.'

It was becoming clear that Curtis was only there for form's sake.

Wycliffe was appreciative. 'My job is to find out who murdered Mrs Kemp and why. To do that I have to look into the details of both her business and private life.'

Curtis spoke for the first time, playing with the cord of his telephone, 'You may rest assured, Superintendent, that there was nothing in her business life to give rise to anything of the sort.'

Beasley cut in. 'Of course I agree with my colleague, but that does not mean that there will be any obstacle to the fullest investigation.'

They were not yet getting down to business. Wycliffe looked out of the window; the view was taken up entirely by part of the south porch of the cathedral; it was almost as though one could reach across the narrow street and touch the biscuit-coloured stone or the leaded panes of the lancet windows.

Wycliffe said, 'The company appears to be very prosperous.'

'It is. Bridget inherited her father's acumen and caution along with his business. The company is sound and, despite the recession, increasingly profitable. We have a policy of planned and gradual expansion, capitalized out of our own resources, and that is proving entirely successful.'

Wycliffe smiled. 'That could be a quote from the chairman's report if you had such a thing. I have a more personal angle in mind. I believe Coast and Country had an interest in the acquisition of Kellycoryk with a view to its development as a leisure centre of some sort.'

For once Beasley was caught off guard, and from the look on Curtis's face it was clear that this was news to him. Beasley recovered his poise. 'I must admit that the idea has been looked at as a vague possibility.'

Wycliffe sat forward in his chair. 'More than that, surely. I understand that Mrs Kemp made a virtual take-over of the estate by the company a condition for providing any assistance towards its upkeep and restoration.'

Beasley, now on his mettle, was terse. 'Of course I cannot say what discussions may or may not have taken place between husband and wife.'

Wycliffe followed up his advantage. 'I quite understand that. But my information is that Mr Kemp came to an arrangement with his wife along those lines shortly before her disappearance and that this was to be the subject of a formal agreement. Did she not mention it to you?'

Beasley shook his head. 'No, I was abroad. But you must see that such an agreement in no way suggests a possible motive for murder – rather the contrary, surely?'

'Unless there is someone determined to prevent such a development taking place.'

A gesture, signifying that this was wild speculation.

Wycliffe changed the subject. 'I understand that you act for

Mrs Kemp in her private capacity also. Presumably she has made a will?'

Beasley hesitated, weighing the situation, then reached a decision. He turned to Curtis. 'I am sure you realize, Ian, that this is a matter which in no way concerns the company . . .'

Curtis did not wait to have it spelt out; he got up with apparent relief. At the door he turned. 'I have some things to do in town. I shall be about half an hour.'

When the door had closed Beasley said, 'You were asking about Bridget's will. Unfortunately there is no will. This may seem incredible to you but in the years since her father died I have tried over and over again to persuade her but to no avail. It was always, "There's plenty of time for that."' The lawyer spread his bony hands in a helpless gesture.

'So who inherits?'

Beasley shrugged. 'The rules governing intestacy are complicated but broadly, in this case, it seems that the beneficiaries will be the husband and his children.'

'But they are his children by a former marriage – not hers.'

'That doesn't affect the position. Speaking as a lawyer, I can see a lot of trouble ahead.'

And speaking as a policeman, Wycliffe could say amen to that.

'And Bridget Kemp's estate includes the company?'

'It will include her holding in the company which amounts to ninety per cent of the share capital.'

Wycliffe had learned more than he bargained for and he was prepared to settle for that. Twice during their discussions they had been interrupted by the chiming of the cathedral clock which seemed to be just above their heads; now, as he stepped out once more into St Mary's Street, the chimes went through their full hourly gamut and the clock struck three.

An interesting three-quarters of an hour but he was not sure where it had got him. And, wherever that was, where did he go from there?

'Oh, it's you.' Molly Bishop came out of the kitchen, wiping her hands on a grubby towel. 'Long time no see. Where've you been this past few days . . . ? Well, don't stand there looking like an undertaker who's lost his corpse. You can come in; but if you're here to see your uncle it's his afternoon at the college.'

'I know.' Crispin was standing in the doorway but he came into the room.

She pushed forward a kitchen chair and sat herself in the rocker. 'Take the weight off your feet. So it's me you've come to see. I suppose things are in a bit of a state at home.'

'Yes.'

'Can you do with a drink? You look as though you need something. There's a can or two of lager in the fridge . . .'

'No . . . No, thank you.'

'I reckon you need something. Is it just to talk to Molly? You're all wound up inside. You've got to learn to let go.' Crispin sat on a kitchen chair, staring into the empty grate, both hands gripped tightly between his knees.

Now she asked him, 'Have the police been since they found out Bridget was shot?'

'They were there this morning, talking to Father.' He stopped, clearly on the point of saying something else.

'Come on! Out with it!'

'I lied to them about what I saw.'

'That won't be a new experience for them.'

'I told them it was a woman who drove Bridget's car away. I made it seem that I thought it was Bridget herself.'

'Well?'

'As I told you before, it wasn't a woman at all, it was Father.'

'You were trying to protect your father. Well, that's natural enough but I know how you feel. Anyway, I expect they'll manage without your help.'

She was looking him over with a critical eye. 'It might do you a bit of good if you found somebody to go to bed with, Crispy. What's the matter with the girls around here? Won't they play?'

Crispin flushed and mumbled, 'She won't have me any more.'

Molly pounced. 'Oh, so there is a she! Then why has she gone off you all of a sudden?'

Crispin lowered his voice so that it was barely audible. 'She says there's something wrong with me, with our family, that we're not right in the head. Her mother thinks so and she will probably stop her coming to work in the house.'

'Ah! So Jane Clemens is your girl. Well, the Clemenses are good ones to talk; Jane's grandmother died in the lunatic asylum, her uncle did time for interfering with little girls, and her aunt goes to Truro hospital for regular treatment, nobody knows quite what for.'

Crispin got up from his chair and moved towards the open door. 'Anyway, I'll do the hen house.'

She called after him; he turned, and was astonished to see her face suffused with tenderness. Her voice too was uncommonly gentle. 'If you go on like this, boy, you're going to make yourself ill. Come upstairs with Molly – and don't worry about Francis, he just thinks of me as an animated mattress anyway.'

Back in the Incident Room Wycliffe found DC Lanyon preparing his report.

'Anything fresh?'

Lanyon was careful. 'Not exactly fresh, sir. I followed up your tip about the first Mrs Kemp's contacts in St Mawes. The man in the gallery who sold her paintings remembers her well enough. He reckons she could have made a real name for herself but there wasn't the output – just the odd one when the mood took her. She would never get together enough work for an exhibition.'

'And the woman who wrote poetry – Holland, wasn't it?'

'June Holland, sir. Yes, she's still around. I didn't know what to make of her story.'

'Try me.'

'She says that the day Julia was drowned they were supposed to have spent together, but Julia didn't turn up.'

'She didn't see her at all that day?'

'No.'

'So what did she think when she heard about the accident?'

'That Julia had forgotten about their arrangement or decided she would rather go sailing. Apparently reliability wasn't her middle name.'

'Yet she had an appointment at St Mawes which she is supposed to have kept.' Curiouser and curiouser. 'Have you found any other contacts she had in St Mawes?'

'Two more, but one, an elderly painter, is dead; the other, a woman, is away at the moment.'

'So Julia definitely did not keep her appointment and you've found nobody who admits to seeing her in St Mawes that day.'

'That's what it amounts to, sir.'

'All right; keep at it. I shall be at Kellycoryk.'

Wycliffe drove down through the village towards the water-front; a dry afternoon after the rain but a high ceiling of cloud. The cafés were serving cream teas to stave off any pangs of hunger there might be before the evening meal.

Wycliffe felt set apart, caught up in a strangely unreal drama of violence among the remnants of an old family struggling to survive. He was uneasy; the logic of the evidence pushed him towards conclusions which conflicted with his instinct. It had emerged that Kemp's first wife, Julia, was not with him on that day five years ago when he and Clare Jordan boarded the boat at Percuil. Now it was clear that she had not kept her appointment in St Mawes either. In fact, there was nothing to show that she had been there.

Had she been on the boat at all? And if not . . .

Bridget, Kemp's second wife, had undoubtedly died by violence. She had been shot, almost certainly, with a little pistol which had come from the junk room in Kellycoryk. Kemp had benefited from the death of his first wife and looked set to do so on a grander scale from the death of his second.

Wycliffe wanted to get closer to the two young Kemps. Like Kersey, he did not believe what the boy had said, and the girl had avoided saying very much at all that was to the point.

He drove along the cliff road and crossed the bridge. The cove was deserted and, under a grey sky, the scene was like a steel engraving; the rocky promontories stood out in silhouette against the silvery plain of the sea. He turned up the drive to the house and as he reached the open ground by the lake he spotted Crispin crossing the alley from the house to the ruins. On an impulse he made straight for the alley and pulled up halfway along it. The boy was still in sight, in fact he had stopped and was looking back.

Wycliffe got out of the car and started after him, only to be surprised by the hard going; the tussocky grass, the brambles, unexpected hollows, and meaningless lumps of masonry defied any attempt at setting a course.

Crispin waited, but did not come towards him. Strange lad; such self-control and lack of spontaneity . . .

Wycliffe, out of breath but anxious to sound relaxed and friendly, said, 'This is a bit of luck, I came to see you.'

Crispin acknowledged the greeting with that colourless courtesy which seemed to come naturally to him.

The boy wore jeans and a waterproof jacket of which the left-hand pocket sagged under some weight.

Wycliffe tried again, looking about them and recovering his breath. 'Interesting place. Have you ever tried to make a plan of the old house?'

'No. Father has one which somebody made a long time ago.'

It was going to be up-hill work. 'I've been reading Jean Scott's book about Kellycoryk and she has a lot to say about the Tudor house.'

'Yes.'

'She mentions a sort of priest's hole under the old building which, she says, still exists.'

There was no response. It was like trying to see through a mirror and Wycliffe was about to revert to being a policeman when the boy said, 'You are talking about Wayne's Closet. Yes, it is still there; it's in the tunnel that takes the stream through to the lake.' He added a moment later and more casually, 'Do you want to see it?'

'I would like to.'

Together they scrambled over the rough ground and reached a small clearing where a flight of worn stone steps led down between moss-grown walls to a heavy padlocked door.

Wycliffe could hear the muffled sound of the stream beneath their feet.

'Down here.'

At the bottom of the steps Crispin went to work with a pick-lock; the door swung open on oiled hinges and they were greeted by the sound of a smooth rush of water. Wycliffe could see a little way into the arching tunnel, the narrow walkway and the gleaming surface of the stream, before it all vanished into the darkness.

Crispin produced a large electric torch from his pocket. 'You'll have to be careful; it's slippery in places.'

'You come here often?'

'No.'

Wycliffe followed the boy along the paved path while the

beam of the torch was lost in the distance. What with the narrowness of the path, the slippery stone slabs underfoot and the inward curve of the walls which made them stoop, he hoped they had not far to go. In fact they soon reached the gap in the wall which he might easily have passed without noticing.

'It's in there.'

Crispin slid through the gap and Wycliffe followed, to find himself in the little cavernous room. The torch beam picked out the rocky walls, the stone slabs of the floor, and the shelf-like recess in one of the walls at about waist level.

'They call it Mayne's Bed because he lived here and slept on that ledge when Sir Richard Grenville and his men were after him in fifteen seventy-seven.' Crispin held the beam steady on the stone slab. 'Of course he was caught later, and executed, but they didn't get him while he was with us.'

The hint of pride in the boy's voice was not lost on Wycliffe but at the moment he was more interested in the little statue of the Virgin and the candlesticks with their stubs of candle.

'Who put all this here?'

'Father.'

'In memory of Mayne?'

'No, of Mother.' He took a box of matches from his pocket, struck one, and lit the candles; they flickered weakly before achieving a steady flame. 'Father comes here to pray. He thinks nobody knows.'

Crispin turned the beam of his torch on to the inscription on the stone slab, not well seen by candlelight. The letters had been laboriously and inexpertly cut, but the inscription was easily legible.

Wycliffe read aloud, 'Julia Constance Kemp, née Harvey, died 13th June 1988, aged 37 years. Pray for her Soul.' He turned to the boy, 'I thought your mother died on the fourteenth.'

Crispin directed his torch beam on to the date. 'That's what he put down.' His manner had the detachment of a guide.

It dawned on Wycliffe that in the moment or two of hesitation after Mayne's Closet was first mentioned the boy had decided that he should see it. He wondered why. More important, what if anything did it mean in the context of the death of Kemp's first wife?

They walked back through the tunnel, Crispin relocked the

door and they climbed the steps. Wycliffe sat on the dwarf wall at the top; there were primroses growing between the stones.

'As I said, I want to talk to you. I know this is painful but I have to look again at the circumstances of your mother's death. Whether we wish it or not people and the press are already making connections between her death and that of your stepmother. Of course I have to be prepared to deal with that situation as it arises.'

Crispin sat on the wall beside him, his manner resigned. 'All right. What do you want me to tell you?'

'I want you to think back to the morning of that day when your mother lost her life. I believe Isobel was away on a school trip and your aunt was staying with a friend in Torquay, so you were here with your parents and Clare Jordan. Is that correct?'

'Yes.'

'Presumably you went to school as usual?'

'Yes.'

'Did you see your mother that morning?'

'No. Clare got breakfast; she often did; Mother didn't get up very early.'

'Did you hear anything of their plans for the day?'

'I knew that Mother was going to St Mawes. I thought it was to see a friend who writes poetry. She mentioned it the night before.'

'Was there any talk of your father and Clare going sailing?'

'I don't remember. I expect I was thinking more about not missing the school bus.'

'And when you got back in the evening?'

'When I got back there was nobody home but that wasn't unusual if Agnes was away. When they came home Father told me what had happened and he got in touch with the school party to break the news to Isobel and arrange for her to come home. He must have telephoned Agnes too because she arrived back next day.'

'Was anything said about your mother having joined the boat at St Mawes?'

'No, I only heard about that afterwards.'

Wycliffe decided to sharpen the probe. 'I'm sorry, but I have to ask you this question: did your mother and father quarrel much?'

'No. I don't think Father ever quarrels.'

'But your mother would get angry with him sometimes?'

'Sometimes; yes.'

'Did you gather that there was any sort of trouble between them on the night before the boat trip?'

'No.'

Wycliffe was puzzled by Crispin's attitude, so apparently detached and uninvolved yet he felt sure that underneath there was intense emotion. Without meaning to he was staring at the boy in a way that many would have found intimidating but the brown eyes met his gaze with no hint of concern, let alone of fear.

He slid off the wall. 'Well, thank you for showing me Mayne's Closet.'

Crispin stood beside him. 'I thought you should see it.'

'Are you coming back to the house?'

'No, I'm going for a walk.'

Chapter Eight

Tuesday 11 May

Wycliffe retrieved his car from the alley and parked in front of the house. There was no other car, so Lucy and the WPC must have given up their search for the little pistol; a needle-in-a-haystack routine anyway. The killer had either pitched it into the lake or was holding on to it for possible future use.

He rang the bell.

The response time seemed to get longer with each visit, and he was beginning to wonder whether there was some fresh crisis when the door was opened by the girl who helped with the housework. Her aggression was obvious.

'I want to speak to Isobel, is she in?'

The girl shrugged. 'I don't know who's in or who's out; they don't tell me.'

'Miss Agnes?'

'She's out.'

'Mr Kemp is in his library?'

'I suppose so.'

'Then please tell him that I shall be upstairs for a little while.'

She was about to make some sharp retort but thought better of it. Instead she said, as though reciting a lesson, 'My family doesn't want me being mixed up in all this. Mother says I shouldn't be working here so I've told them I'm leaving.'

Wycliffe looked at her as though she had not spoken. 'If you will just give Mr Kemp my message.'

In modern police investigation, every move, every interview, every scrap of evidence is recorded in the pious hope that through processes of evaluation, comparison and correlation (largely carried out by computers) indicators will emerge to guide the investigator in the way he should go.

Wycliffe did not knock the system, it was immensely useful;

apart from anything else, in most cases it guaranteed that bland pre-digested diet preferred by the CPS and the courts. But for cases like the present one, involving a small group of closely interrelated people, Wycliffe believed that it was essential to see life through their eyes, to stand in their shoes, to become familiar with their backgrounds and aware of the constraints and antagonisms which informed their relationships.

That was what he tried to do and he was making progress. Now he was about to snoop around the upper floor and attics of the old house and if he was alone, so much the better.

He began with the attics, which he had not yet seen. At the east end of the first floor corridor near where the back stairs came up and Isobel and her brother had their rooms, another staircase, steep and narrow, led upwards. This was uncarpeted and so was the long, narrow passage at the top. On either side of the passage plank doors opened into rooms where, in other days, the servants had slept.

He decided to take a look in each, though Lucy and her assistant in their hunt-the-thimble routine must have given them at least a cursory glance. There were seven doors; the first four attics, two on each side, were empty except for buckets and enamel bowls strategically placed under damp patches. The windows were so thick with grime that it was difficult to see out and some panes had been replaced by plywood.

Opening the door of the next room – one at the back of the house – he had a surprise. It was twice the size of the others, the two dormer windows were reasonably clean and fully glazed. There were paint-stained floorboards, a couple of easels and a painter's donkey: no prizes for guessing that the room had been a painter's studio. There was even a paint table with rows of tubes laid out ready for use, and a stoneware jar holding a collection of brushes.

'Were you looking for something?' Isobel must have followed him up the stairs and was standing in the doorway.

'Was this your mother's studio?'

She nodded. 'They've been in here this morning.'

'Who keeps it like this?'

'I do. When Mother died they let me bring all her clothes up here.' She gestured vaguely to a couple of cupboards which occupied one wall. 'Everything else of hers was up here anyway.'

He was disturbed by the change in the girl; she had lost her
aggression; vitality had gone out of her and she looked at him
with dull resignation.

'Do you mind if I look around?'

A gesture.

Between the windows there were shelves crammed with
books: a miniature library on the history of art and a mixed
bag of fiction and biography.

Wycliffe looked around the room. No desk, no filing drawers;
in fact, very few drawers of any sort. 'Surely your mother must
have left papers – letters, that sort of thing?'

'She didn't leave much. Mother wasn't one for keeping
things.'

'And what she did leave?'

Isobel looked at him intently for a moment or two, then
turned away. There was a catch in her voice. 'I wish I could
trust you.'

Wycliffe was moved; for an instant this was his own daughter
a few years earlier with something on her mind, something to
tell.

He said, 'I will tell you exactly how far you can trust me,
Isobel, then you must make up your own mind. It is my job to
find out who killed your stepmother and why. It is also my job
to explain, if I can, circumstances surrounding your mother's
death which seem to cast doubt on the idea that it was accidental. All I can say is that anything you tell me will remain confi-
dential as long as it is not directly relevant to what I have to
do.'

There was a sound of heavy footsteps on the stairs leading to
the attics, then on the bare boards of the passage outside. It was
strange. They stood, waiting, looking at each other, until the
footsteps ceased and Roger Kemp stood in the open doorway.
The situation had features of a confrontation, but it was nothing
of the sort; Roger was behaving more like an intruder. He
looked from one to the other, and at the room which had been
his wife's, in mild astonishment and muttered, 'I had no
idea . . .'

Wycliffe wondered how long it was since he had last seen the
inside of this room.

Kemp repeated, 'No idea . . .' Then, recovering himself, he

turned to Wycliffe. 'They told me you were up here, but I see that Isobel is looking after you so . . .' His voice trailed off. He stood his ground for a little longer, then turned away. They waited while his footsteps receded along the passage and down the stairs.

Isobel looked at Wycliffe and her expression seemed to say, 'You see?' Then, aloud. 'Is it possible that he . . . ?' She did not finish her question but the incident seemed to have given her confidence. She said, 'Mother had a lover.' And a moment later she added, 'She was pregnant by him when she died.'

'She told you this?'

'No! Just now you asked about her papers. Well, among them was a notebook in which she scribbled down odd things that happened, things that were on her mind, things that she intended to do . . . It wasn't a diary but something like that.'

Wycliffe nodded. 'And in it she mentioned her pregnancy?'

'Several times. And she was always referring to "Pasto" as she called him. I suppose it was her pet name for the man. I don't know who he was.'

She spoke baldly and Wycliffe realized the effort it was costing her.

'Was she distressed about her pregnancy?'

'No, she seemed pleased. At one point what she wrote seemed to mean that she was intending to leave Father and live with the other man, but then there were difficulties.'

'You still have this notebook?'

She flushed. 'No, I burned it.'

'So you've known about this ever since your mother died?'

'No, I found the little book less than a year ago when I had all the books out of the shelves because some of them seemed to be going mouldy. It was hidden at the back.'

'And that's what started you asking questions.'

'I wanted to know if Mother had taken her own life because there seemed no other way out, or if she had been deliberately . . .' Her voice let her down but a moment later she added with emphasis, 'I still want to know.'

Wycliffe was well aware of what all this had cost the girl and he did not want to prolong her distress but there was something else he needed to know. 'I suppose you know of the little shrine in Mayne's Closet?'

She nodded. 'So Crispy has told you about that. I'm glad.'

Wycliffe sat in his chair and brooded.

Kemp, a man with an obsession. Had that obsession cost the lives of his two wives . . . ? There was no real evidence concerning the first – and no body. But the second? If Kemp had killed his second wife what could have persuaded him to drive her body to Kellycoryk and leave it there for hours before finally disposing of it?

A good question to which there was no obvious answer.

Wycliffe was alone in his makeshift office and the little room was catching the early evening sun, making him feel drowsy.

But Roger was not the only one with a motive. Under the provisions of his father's will if Kellycoryk was *sold*, Roger would receive half the proceeds while Francis, Agnes, and Clare Jordan had one-sixth each. But if the property was leased as proposed, any possible carve-up would be indefinitely postponed.

Although Kellycoryk as a unit might be a liability, broken up into lots: the hundred and fifty acres of farmland, fifty of woodland, the lake, the house, Chylathva, the cottages and cove, would surely bring in enough to make a one-sixth share attractive . . .

Commonplace greed is the motive for most crimes, from theft to murder, but he could see little that was commonplace in the events at Kellycoryk . . . *And there is nothing commonplace about madness!* The words which he had come across somewhere recently seemed to erupt into his thoughts.

He was in a strange mood. In those few cases in which he had become personally and deeply involved there had come a time when, without any particular regard for the evidence, indeed without much conscious thought of any sort, he had reached a conclusion which had served him as a guiding principle through the rest of the case.

There's nothing commonplace about madness.

Fragments of memory, phrases read or spoken, scenes witnessed, even the odd word or gesture, seemed suddenly to correlate in his mind, to form the outline of a pattern and to suggest a coherent view of what really mattered.

Molly, speaking of Francis: 'I live here with him and, like all the Kemps, he's never grown up.' And later. 'Of course he's a Kemp; they're all dreamers. Frankie's thing is being a great painter. If he'd only settle for being good . . .'

And Clare Jordan: 'You might say I took the opportunity to escape . . . life at Kellycoryk was a strange experience. You felt cut off, isolated from normality by a whole system of ideas, assumptions, prejudices . . .'

Isobel: 'I've had enough of this! You don't understand!'

And Crispin, who said very little . . . Perhaps too little . . .

Then a visual memory of Roger Kemp lying back in his chair, staring at the ceiling with Coryk curled up among the papers on his work table.

And two, more moving, visual experiences of that very afternoon: in Mayne's Closet, standing by Crispin as the boy shone his torch on the words inscribed by his father on a memorial stone to his mother.

And later, in what had been Julia Kemp's studio – that fleeting moment when Kemp had faced his daughter across the floor as though across some unbridgeable gulf, muttering to himself, 'I had no idea . . . No idea.'

Wycliffe became aware that he was stiff and uncomfortable in his chair. It was evening, the light was golden. Time to go home.

He arrived back at the cottage and pulled off the track to park. He cut the engine but did not immediately get out of the car. The sun must be low over the Nare, the sky was almost cloudless and the sea shone. Already there were lights in the cottage and he could see Helen moving around, perhaps laying the table for supper. In a moment or two she would look up and see him but for once he was reluctant to return to the domestic routine.

At least he was clearer in his mind about things that had previously confused him. The crime he had been called in to solve was the murder of Bridget Kemp, and he was becoming convinced that it had little to do with wills, with Coast and Country, with whether or not the Kemps would continue at Kellycoryk, with who might gain or who might lose if this or that course were adopted. Rather it was an explosion of hate . . . Perhaps not even that; but a release of inner tensions which had become insupportable.

But who was suffering these suppressed and insupportable tensions that could find release only in violence? Roger? His brother Francis? He had to admit that to him the Kemp brothers seemed essentially weak and ineffective, bumbling rather than vicious. But Isobel? Agnes? Crispin?

Helen had spotted him sitting in the car; she waved. Time to go indoors.

Pork spare ribs after marinating in a witches' brew of apple, onion, lemon, and garlic, grilled and served with mushrooms and sauté potatoes. Wycliffe gave the occasion his seal of approval with another bottle of the light and fruity Barsac.

They talked about the cove and the remnants of an almost feudal relationship which had survived into the present century and received its death blow in the aftermath of the First World War.

Helen said, 'But five of the cottages are still occupied by families who owe their tenancy to former service with the Kemps. Mrs Pascoe, who has the cottage by the bridge, told me that her husband's family had been at Kellycoryk almost as long as the Kemps. He himself was employed there as a boy, but now he works for a builder in the village.'

When Wycliffe set out on his walk the sun had gone down and the sea had taken on a translucent greenish hue. By the time he reached the cottage by the bridge he knew that he had already decided to call on the Pascoes.

There were lights on upstairs and down, and muted pop music, all enveloping, pulsated in the air. He walked up the path and knocked. His knock was answered by a woman with whom he already had a nodding acquaintance. She was fortyish, pleasant, and he remembered that she walked with a slight limp.

'I wondered if you and your husband could spare me a few minutes?'

'Mr Wycliffe . . . ! Come in, do! But you must take us as you find us.'

He followed her into the living room. 'This is Jim, my husband.' Jim had the newspaper spread on the table among the supper dishes, a brawny man with a dark moustache. The raucous pop music, dominant now, came from upstairs.

He said, 'Our two girls, twelve and fifteen; they say they can't do their homework without that row.' He raised his voice. 'Turn that thing off, Jean! We've got company.'

Peace descended like the heavenly dove and Jim said, 'There! Isn't it nice when they turn it off?'

It was Wycliffe who felt at a disadvantage. 'As your cottage is so close to the bridge I wondered if either of you heard a car arriving at or leaving Kellycoryk on the night Mrs Kemp disappeared?'

Pascoe looked at his wife. 'Ask her. I go to bed to sleep.'

Mrs Pascoe nodded. 'Yes, I often hear Mrs Kemp's car when she comes in late and I did that night. I can't say when it was exactly but she woke me. Then, some time later, when I'd got off to sleep again I heard a car driving away – up the hill out of the cove. O' course I couldn't say whether it was the same car.'

This was a bonus. It was not what he had come for; that was more difficult if he was to avoid stirring up gossip. He said, trying to sound casual, 'I've become interested in Kellycoryk and, knowing that your family were for so long part of the place, I thought I would like to talk to you.'

Jim folded his newspaper. 'You're welcome, Mister, but I can't tell you anything about the family as it is now. I've not worked there for more'n ten years, and then the first Mrs Kemp was still with us.'

Wycliffe said, 'It's not so much the people as the place that I was hoping to learn something about, in particular the old house and the tunnel. Perhaps I should say that I've read Jean Scott's book and that I've seen the tunnel and Mayne's Closet.'

Pascoe grinned. 'You must be somebody special; but there, I suppose you are.'

'I have to admit that I'm interested. Is it supposed to be some sort of secret?'

'I don't know about secret exactly, but the Kemps don't like it talked about. God knows why after all this time, but that's how they are.'

Pascoe looked at his wife, then at Wycliffe, and seemed to decide. 'Well, everybody round here knows the story and there's no reason why you shouldn't. It seems that the old house, the Tudor house, used to get flooded pretty regular, and a certain John Kemp, way back in the seventeen-fifties, decided to deepen the tunnel. To do it he drafted in men from the mines, and the bed of the stream was lowered by four feet, say about six feet below what is now the walkway level.'

Pascoe, warming to his story, tilted back his chair. 'Now this John Kemp was a bit of an antiquarian and, through his work on the tunnel, he got interested in Mayne's Closet. The story goes that in that sort of built-in stone chest they call Mayne's Bed, he found a collection of church silver rightly belonging to St Endel church. It must have bin hidden there long before to keep it out of the hands of the King's men an' somehow it got overlooked when the Pope came out on top again with Queen Mary.' Pascoe looked at Wycliffe. 'You don't need me to go on from there.'

Wycliffe finished for him. 'You're saying that more than two centuries ago John Kemp found the little hoard and disposed of it on the black market of the time.'

Pascoe chuckled. 'Anyway, that's the story that's come down through the families in the cove. All I can say is, if it's true, the Kemps had better luck then than they've had since . . .' He broke off. 'Ah, that looks better!'

Mrs Pascoe had come in from the kitchen with cans of bitter and glasses. 'We sometimes have a glass about now if we got company.'

It was after ten when Wycliffe left, and he was seen off at the gate by husband and wife. Nice people. He felt guilty about something without being quite sure what.

The sky had clouded over and it was very dark, only the sea shone dimly and he had to pick his way over the bridge and along the track back home.

Tuesday night and Wednesday morning 11/12 May

Wycliffe had a restless night. A freakish notion which had been lurking on the fringes of his thoughts was beginning to acquire a sort of credibility and he was impatient for morning and the chance to try it out. Caution would have to be his watchword or he ran the risk of falling flat on his face in the proverbial mire.

He had to deal with Helen's plaintive question. 'Can't you sleep?' And later, with her resigned diagnosis. 'It must be those spare ribs.' He noted this second observation at a quarter-past two. Then he did sleep, and dreamed a dream which sometimes turned up with appropriate variations when he was under stress. He was a young constable again, a greenhorn in the witness box, being cross-examined by defending counsel, cold and supercilious: 'These events took place on the thirteenth of the month. You agree with that date, Constable?'

'Yes, sir.'

A pause while counsel surveys the courtroom to let the point go home, then, 'Are you possessed of second sight or some other means by which you are enabled to foresee the future?'

'No.'

'Then how does it come about that your notebook record of the occurrence is dated the twelfth?'

By shortly after six he was awake again. He eased himself out of bed and went downstairs, made coffee, and walked on the shore. No sign of Harvey though his Deux-Chevaux was parked by the cottage. It was misty, not actually raining, but wetting. He was restless. It would be another two hours at least before he could get to work without giving too much of a build-up to a possible fiasco. Resigned, he went back to the cottage, found Helen's Trollope in the window seat, opened it at random and started to read. At half-past seven when Helen came downstairs she found him in his chair fast asleep.

At nine he was closeted with Kersey and Lucy Lane. 'I don't want to ask permission; I think we must go for a warrant.'

At eleven o'clock, in two cars, they were on their way up the drive at Kellycoryk. Wycliffe was in the first car, with Lucy Lane, Kersey and Fox. A uniformed constable and a technician called Knowles, who knew about locks, travelled in the second car. Avoiding the front of the house, the two cars parked in the alley which led to the yard and marked the boundary between the 'new' house and the ruins of the old.

When they were all out, Wycliffe said, 'I'm leaving it to you, Lucy. Take the constable with you, tell Kemp that we propose to investigate Mayne's Closet, show him the warrant, and leave it at that.'

The four men, Fox with his camera gear, the technician with his case of tools, set out over the sodden grass, picking their way between the maze of walls. It was raining now, a thin rain drifting before a fitful breeze. When they reached the steps which led down to the padlocked door they could hear the water, a muffled, unremitting scurry of sound. Knowles made short work of the lock, the door opened, and daylight reached feebly into the darkness of the tunnel. Kersey switched on a powerful hand lamp.

Wycliffe said, 'Mind your heads and watch out for your feet, it may be slippery.'

The confined stream moved with a smooth rush, its sound echoing beneath the arching walls. Kersey's lamp made swirling patterns of light on the rippling surface.

Wycliffe led the way. 'It's not far.'

They reached the narrow entrance to Mayne's Closet. 'I want you in there first, Fox. Photographs of the place before we disturb it. Make sure that the inscription on the slate is readable.'

Kersey said, 'The things we do for a living.'

Fox inserted himself into the cavity. Kersey passed him the lamp, and Fox set about becoming acquainted with the amenities of Mayne's Closet while the others waited in darkness.

Intermittent clicks, burrs and flashes punctuated the next few minutes before Fox said, 'I think that's it.'

He was joined by Wycliffe and Knowles where, at least, they could stand upright.

Wycliffe went to the recess. 'I think there must be a cavity under the slates; lift them without damaging them if you can.'

After the fashion of good tradesmen the world over, with slow deliberation, Knowles removed the statue of the Virgin and the two candlesticks to a place of safety in one corner. Then, selecting a chisel from his bag, he inserted the blade beneath the slate at one end and began tapping it with his hammer, working along the whole length and back again several times until, gently, the mortar was shaken loose. This done, he lifted the slates undamaged and rested them on the floor.

Wycliffe's cavity (he felt a proprietorial interest) was narrower than might have been expected because the supporting wall consisted of foot-thick slabs of granite. There was a strong, almost choking smell of decay, dank and putrid. The cavity seemed to be stuffed with black, rotting straw.

Wycliffe picked up a short crowbar from Knowles's kit and,

directing the light into the cavity, he began, gently, to push the straw to one end. At a depth of about a foot he uncovered the staring eye-sockets of a human face.

He turned away. 'All right; let's get outside.'

Fox went first through the gap, followed by Knowles and his tools, with Wycliffe bringing up the rear. Waiting on the walkway in darkness Kersey was unaware of what, if anything, had been found.

Wycliffe shepherded them back to the entrance and up the steps into the open air with, for more reasons than one, a sense of relief, but his manner was terse and sombre. 'I think we've found Julia Kemp but now it's a matter for Franks and the professionals.'

It was still raining, gossamer threads of rain; but there had been a spectator. Crispin was moving off, unhurried, and, apparently, untroubled by whether he was seen or not.

Wycliffe should have been pleased. Earlier he was concerned at the possibility that he was making a fool of himself but now his hunch had paid off and there was good reason to hope that he would soon know what had really happened to the first Mrs Kemp. But any satisfaction was mingled with a gut feeling that all this was bringing him no nearer to solving the murder of Bridget Kemp.

On the car phone he enlisted his experts.

Chapter Nine

Wednesday morning 12 May

Roger was at his table, the ritual papers and books spread out in front of him. In the midst of it all Coryk slept, disturbed now and then by feline dreams, or by indigestion. But it was days since Roger had added anything significant to the heap of manuscript in the open filing tray.

Outside it was overcast and raining; in the library an ancient desk lamp shed its yellow light over the littered table and shone on Coryk's glossy black fur. For several days now, Roger had kept a small glass by his hand and a two-litre bottle of cheap red wine on the floor by his chair. From time to time he would top up the glass, his movements surreptitious, although there was no one to see.

He felt trapped, finally overtaken by the past. For five years he had lived with the knowledge that it was possible, at any time . . . Now that time had come and in circumstances which he could never have imagined even in his worst moments. There was a tap at the door; it opened, and Crispin came in. Roger could not remember the last occasion when Crispin had come into the library, or sought him out anywhere. The boy came to stand by the table, his pallor jaundiced by the lamplight. He wore jeans and a nondescript jacket, he was rarely seen in anything else, and he seemed totally indifferent to the weather. Now, jeans and jacket were darkened by rain, his hair was plastered to his head, and drops of moisture glistened on his forehead.

Roger tried to sound ordinary. 'You're wet, Crispy.'

Crispin said, 'They've been in Mayne's Closet for an hour. They've just come out.'

Roger shook his head like a man in a trance but said nothing.

Crispin went on, 'You know what they've found.'

Father and son stared at each other, wordless.

Any further exchange was prevented by another tap at the door, and Agnes came in, white faced and sombre. 'The police again.'

Wycliffe and the dour inspector who had brought the news that Bridget had been shot.

'Detective Superintendent Wycliffe and Detective Inspector Kersey.'

Wycliffe said, 'Mr Kemp, I have to tell you that remains which we believe to be human have been found in the recessed portion of Mayne's Closet.

'Obviously there will be an inquiry to establish the identity of those remains and how they came to be there. If you have any comment or explanation which you wish to offer, we are here to listen. On the other hand you may prefer to wait until we have more positive information.'

Roger did not know what he had expected from the police, he had refused to allow himself to speculate, but this was not it. Wycliffe was mild-mannered and matter-of-fact; even his hard-faced companion did not behave aggressively ... And there were no uniforms. Roger fumbled with his papers while choosing his words; finally he said, 'Yes ... That will be best.'

Crispin looked on, his face expressionless.

Wycliffe continued, dryly official. 'In order to assist our inquiries we shall need photographs of your first wife with any details of distinguishing physical characteristics which you are able to provide.'

Roger looked about him as though in search of help which he failed to find, then he said, 'Agnes ... Yes, Agnes will give you what you want ... And John Harvey ... John is Julia's brother – and he's a doctor ...'

They left Kellycoryk finally with half a dozen photographs and a few details of Julia's physique. Outside, Kersey said, 'I know all that I've said about that guy but I still don't know what to make of him. He could fit almost anywhere in my book between a well-intentioned if self-centred bungler and a psychotic killer. But whatever he is, he was expecting to be led away in handcuffs.'

When they were getting into the car Wycliffe, perhaps a little on the defensive, said, 'I don't want this to go off at half-cock, Doug. When we move we must be sure of our ground.'

*   *   *

They were lunching at the New Inn, Kersey, Lucy Lane and
Wycliffe. There were not many customers for Mrs Sara's lamb
stew, which was a pity. But it meant they could speak freely.

Kersey said, 'I don't understand what put you on to it.'

Wycliffe wasn't quite sure himself and he had no intention of
trying to rationalize the hotch-potch of experiences and notions
which had led him to the stone chest.

He said, 'You probably noticed that although Julia Kemp
was supposed to have drowned on the fourteenth of June, the
inscription on the slate slab, cut by Roger, puts her death at the
thirteenth.'

'A mistake.'

'I thought so at first but then it occurred to me that she might
really have died on the thirteenth and the story of her drowning
could have been a cover-up . . . I mean, when a body is found
an inquiry is inevitable, but in a case of drowning nobody is all
that surprised if the body fails to turn up.'

Kersey paused with his fork halfway to his lips. 'A cover-up?
Are you suggesting that Kemp not only murdered his first wife
but that there wasn't even the trappings of an accident at sea?'

'I think it's possible, even likely, that Julia Kemp was already
dead when Roger and Clare Jordan set out for their boat trip
on the morning of the fourteenth. The boat trip was a charade.
Julia had an appointment in St Mawes which she never kept.
She did not board the boat with her husband and Clare Jordan at
Percuil. Neither, in my opinion, did she join them at St Mawes.'

Lucy said, 'All this means that Clare Jordan was his
accomplice.'

Wycliffe shrugged.

'But if what you are saying is true, surely Kemp would have
taken the trouble to get his date right.'

Wycliffe said, 'I think that can be explained, but I'd rather it
waited until we have proof that the body we found in Mayne's
Closet really is that of Julia Kemp.' Abruptly, he turned to Lucy
Lane. 'Do Roman Catholics bury their dead in a special cemetery
or a specially allocated part of a cemetery?'

'I don't think either. As far as I know, it's simply a question
of the ground being consecrated. Why the sudden interest, sir?'

'Would you say that Mayne's Closet was consecrated
ground?'

Lucy was intrigued. 'You would have to get a professional opinion on that. I can imagine some ecclesiastical committee sitting for weeks to decide it. My father's customers are mainly Methodists – if they are anything – but most of his flock opt for cremation anyway.' Lucy, with characteristic objectivity.

Kersey was finding it all difficult to take. 'Shouldn't we at least be pulling in Kemp and the Jordan woman for questioning?'

'They won't run away.'

The afternoon brought watery sunshine. By four o'clock there was a flurry of activity in the ruins of Tudor Kellycoryk, probably more than at any time since the old house became a quarry for materials from which to build the new. With the approval of the coroner the body was to be removed for identification and post-mortem examination.

Cars, and a plain van, were lined up in the alleyway between the house and the ruins. Four men, all kitted out in protective clothing, picked their discriminating way down the steps, and through the tunnel to the reclusion of Mayne's Closet and the grisly remains which had been hidden under his stone bed. One of the men was Franks, the pathologist, two others were scientific officers from Forensic, and the fourth was Fox with his camera and lighting equipment. Wycliffe had put in an appearance to satisfy protocol but proceeded no further than the entrance to the tunnel. Twenty minutes went by before Franks, still in full kit, complete with mask, rejoined him.

'You do find me some nice jobs, Charles. Sometimes I think I would have done better as a sewage operative if that is the politically correct job description. I can't tell you much until we get her out. She's been there some time – years, probably, but it's not going to be easy to make an assessment.'

Franks brooded, thinking aloud. 'The body is clothed, and in what amounts to a sealed stone coffin. Insect activity would have been minimal . . . Unless that bloody straw made a difference . . . The temperature in the chamber probably doesn't vary much either side of eight to ten degrees . . . The humidity is hardly a factor if the coffin was sealed . . .'

Franks sighed. 'On balance I'd say the conditions favour preservation, but we shall have to see. Anyway, identification shouldn't be a problem and it should be possible to establish the cause of death without too much difficulty. You're expecting this to be the body of the first Mrs Roger Kemp?'

'I shall be surprised if it turns out to be anybody else.'

'And she went missing five years ago so that gives me somewhere to start.'

Two men in white came out of the tunnel and went up the steps.

Franks said, 'They've gone to fetch the shell so we shan't be long now.'

Wycliffe said, 'I've arranged for Dr Harvey to attend for identification purposes. Although he's a doctor, as the dead woman's brother it will be a pretty gruesome business for him, but he's agreed.'

News of the discovery had leaked out and half a dozen reporters, four men and two women, some with cameras, had tramped through the ruins to the top of the stone steps where a uniformed man held the pass.

The presence of Wycliffe was an unexpected bonus and they gathered round.

'What's the story? Another body?'

'There's no story yet. All I can tell you is that this morning a body was found in a chamber off the tunnel which carries the stream beneath the old house.'

'Mayne's Closet?' From one of the women.

'You've evidently done your homework. Yes. Actually the body was concealed in a sort of stone chest known as Mayne's Bed.'

'How long has it been there?'

'That is what the pathologist will try to find out.'

One of the men looked suspicious. 'What's all this about Mayne's Closet? Are we talking about ancient history or another crime? I mean, you wouldn't be here if they were just digging up some corpse from way back.'

'We shall know more after the post-mortem. Until then . . .'

That evening the Wycliffes departed from routine and had their meal at a little restaurant in Portloe which, with a disregard for furnishing and décor that was almost French, concentrated on the food and wine. With a certain feeling of smugness they walked there and back, so avoiding the need to nominate a sacrificial abstainer to drive the car.

On their homeward trek, above and ahead of them, was a

cloudless turquoise sky, but behind them, over the Nare, the sunset was hidden by a bank of dense cloud. Wycliffe, who liked to sound like the Ancient Mariner, said, 'Rain tomorrow.'

Thursday morning 13 May

But the day dawned with limpid clarity; high, pale cloud obscured the sun, and the sea was a silvery plain; only the smallest ripples broke along the shore.

The breakfast-time radio news had the story: 'At Kellycoryk in Cornwall, home of the Kemp family, police yesterday afternoon discovered the body of a woman concealed in a subterranean stone chest in the ruins of the old house. The police are already investigating the murder of Mrs Bridget Kemp, wife of the present owner of the estate, whose body was recovered from the sea last Monday. She had been shot through the head.'

Wycliffe arrived at the Incident Room while parents, in cars and on foot were delivering their offspring to the school, and elderly visitors, on early-summer packages, collected their newspapers from the post office. But Kersey too turned up with a selection of the newspapers. 'They go as far as they can without actually saying that this is the body of Kemp's first wife.'

Kersey was in a contentious mood. 'I suppose, sir, that we now sit about waiting until Franks delivers himself of what we already know. In the old days we'd have had Kemp and the Jordan woman banged up by now.'

There were times when Wycliffe could be irritated by Kersey's moods and this was one. 'No, we do not sit about waiting, we try for a breakthrough in the Bridget Kemp case where we are sure of our facts. Bridget Kemp was shot a week ago and it's three days since her body was recovered, but we've not got very far. There's little doubt that she was shot at Hendra Croft and driven to Kellycoryk in the load space of her estate car. The car remained in the alleyway beside the house for well over an hour. Isobel says she saw it from her window with the driver's door wide open; her brother claims that he saw it being driven off by someone he took to be a woman. I've no doubt the car was there, though I don't necessarily believe the young Kemps' versions of what they saw. In any case, we've nothing to suggest who the killer was or how he or she got to Hendra Croft.'

Kersey was taken aback. 'But surely if Kemp was responsible for the death of his first wife—'

Wycliffe cut him short. 'There is no real evidence that Kemp killed anybody, but if you believe that he did then you should go all out at finding factual evidence which will justify holding him. I think you might be wasting your time. Kemp is a sitting duck and a bit of a fool, but there are other targets.'

Wycliffe looked at his old friend and his manner softened. 'We go back a long way, Doug, and times have changed. I suggest we keep the broad view for a bit longer, at least until we understand the link, if any, between her killing and the death of her predecessor.'

Kersey's grin was sheepish. 'You're the boss.'

Lucy Lane, witness to the exchange, was having a rare glimpse of the depth of the relationship which existed between these two so different men.

They were interrupted by the telephone. 'Dr Franks for you, sir.' Franks too, had started early.

'I tried to get you at the cottage, Charles, but Helen said you'd already left. I'm having the day off and I want to get in some sailing. I've worked half the night on your latest offering.

'Your body, Charles, was female, aged between thirty-five and forty, dark-haired, medium height – about one metre sixty-five. From what evidence remains, including the clothing, I would say that she was of medium build; about sixty kilos, stripped. As far as I can tell her skull and facial bone structure are consistent with the photographs. If necessary we can use dental records and there is quite a bit of soft tissue remaining.'

'Clothing?'

'I'm coming to that. She was wearing a cotton nightdress and a brushed nylon dressing gown. Nothing on her feet. She wore a plain gold wedding ring and she had a gold cross on a chain about her neck. I should add that Dr Harvey is in no doubt that it is the body of his sister. He was very distressed.'

'Cause of death?'

Franks decided that he was being pressurized. 'Don't try to rush me, Charles! However, your woman seems to have died of a severely depressed fracture of the skull in the neighbourhood of the parietal/occipital suture.'

'A blow?'

'You may not have noticed, Charles, but a blow of some sort is the usual means by which skulls become fractured. The possibilities are that she was struck by someone, that she fell, or that she was pushed.'

'Was the impact with a smooth surface?'

'No, in my opinion with a sharpish edge.'

'So, your informed guess?'

'I don't know how informed I can call it, but in my view the likelihood is that she fell.'

'Fair enough. Anything else?'

'The way in which the body was positioned in that chest thing probably means that it was placed there after rigor had passed off, probably twenty-four hours or more after death.'

Wycliffe was saying his thanks when Franks played his trump: 'Don't you want to know that she was pregnant?'

'Ah!'

'You don't seem all that surprised.'

Wycliffe was evasive. 'Well, it's not unheard of in a married woman of thirty-seven, is it? How long?'

'Sixteen weeks or thereabouts. Anyway, I'm off sailing; if you find any more save 'em for another day.'

So Isobel's story had not been fantasy.

Kersey was unimpressed. 'Apart from her pregnancy he's told us nothing much we didn't already know. At least we can get going, but what's it to be? What sort of charge can we bring?'

'For a start, the most you can expect is conspiracy to conceal a death and/or pervert the course of justice. And a nit-picking lawyer might blow holes through either or both. Let's hear what the pair of them have to say under formal questioning.

'I want you to invite – yes, *invite* in the first instance – Kemp to come with you to sub-division for questioning in connection with the death of his first wife. Bring Clive Lanyon in on this.

'Lucy Lane and WPC Rees will do the same with Clare Jordan. At this stage they will both be helping us with our inquiries. We'll keep it that way for the time being. I shall join Lucy at sub-division.'

Kersey said, 'Do I mention Julia's pregnancy?'

Wycliffe, placatory, said, 'You don't need my advice, Doug. Play it by ear.'

*　　*　　*

DC Lanyon pressed the recorder button and recited the preliminary incantation. 'This interview begins at 11.05. Present Detective Inspector Kersey and Detective Constable Lanyon. Let me
remind you that you are not under arrest and that you do not
have to say anything but what you do say . . .'

Roger Kemp, in a grubby shirt and a crumpled suit, sat
in the little windowless interview room looking about him
with vague unfocused eyes like a man newly awakened from
sleep.

Kersey opened the questioning. 'With the finding of your first
wife's body in Mayne's Closet do you now admit that the
account you gave of her being lost overboard on a boating trip
was a fabrication?'

It seemed that the question took a little time to sink in but
the answer when it came was definite. 'Yes.'

'I must remind you again that you are entitled to have a legal
adviser present at this interview.'

'I don't want a lawyer.'

'So your wife was already dead on the fourteenth of June
when that trip took place?'

'Yes.'

'When did she die?'

'The night before.'

'Think carefully before you answer this question. Were you
present when she died?'

'Yes.'

'Will you describe the circumstances?'

A profound sigh and a long pause. In the silence they could
hear the traffic on the roundabout outside the station. 'We were
in the bedroom, going to bed, and there was a quarrel.'

'What was the quarrel about?'

Roger spread his plump soft hands in a helpless gesture. 'I
don't know . . . Couples do quarrel.'

'Was it anything to do with your wife being pregnant?'

Roger winced as though he had been struck. '*What?*'

'The pathologist says that your wife was fifteen or sixteen
weeks pregnant when she died. Didn't you know?'

A long pause. 'Yes, I did know. She told me that night. I
didn't think they could tell, not after all this time . . .' He added
after a moment, 'You see, it was not my child.'

'She told you that too?'

Roger looked at Kersey's rubbery, expressive features and looked quickly away. He mumbled, 'She had no need to tell me; we had had no relations of that kind for nearly a year.'

'So that was what the quarrel was about?'

Asking questions of Roger was like interrogating a computer, one watched the changing patterns flicker across the screen until a resolution was achieved.

'No, it was because she wanted me to divorce her.'

'So that she could marry this other man?'

'Yes ... I would have accepted the child as mine but that was not enough.'

In an identical little room, adjoining, Clare Jordan sat, apparently at ease. Her hair was perfectly controlled; she must have had a recent visit to the hairdresser's. No tinting; those grey streaks testified to wisdom and experience. She wore a plain cornflower-blue frock with a string of pearls, and she carried a white pigskin handbag. Middle-aged virginity tastefully preserved and packaged.

Wycliffe and Lucy Lane were about to tax her with questions not very different to those put by Kersey to Kemp. After the prescribed ritual and a few questions to lead in, Wycliffe asked, 'Was Julia Kemp with you on the boating trip?'

'No.'

'She was already dead?'

'Yes.'

'When did she die?'

'The night before.'

'Were you present when she died?'

'Yes.'

'Will you describe the circumstances?'

There was a brief pause while she set her ideas in order. She was a model witness, no word wasted. 'At that time Roger, his wife, his fourteen-year-old son and I were the only ones in the house. At something after eleven, when the boy and I were both in bed, I heard a quarrel going on in their bedroom which was next to mine.'

'The room used by Roger Kemp and his wife?'

'Their bedroom – yes.'

Wycliffe asked, 'Were quarrels between Roger Kemp and his wife frequent?'

'No, but they did occur from time to time, and when they did they tended to become violent – on Julia's side, that is. I have never known Roger raise a hand to anyone.'

After a moment of hesitation she added, 'I knew the risks if Julia became hysterical and when I thought that point was being reached I decided to interfere. I slipped on a dressing gown and went to their room.' She paused, as though reliving the moment in her memory, then: 'When I entered the room they were both standing between the bed and the old fireplace. Julia was clinging to Roger with one hand and hitting him with the other. At the same time she was hissing abuse.'

Lucy said, 'Was Roger resisting?'

'No. But as I came into the room he took hold of both her arms and forced her away from him, he held her for a moment, then he released her. There was no violence in what he did, but as he let go of her arms she just crumpled up; she seemed to slip backwards and, as she fell, she struck her head against the corner of the marble mantelpiece.

'Of course I went to help Julia but at first Roger seemed paralysed with shock. He just stood looking down at her, where she lay with her head in the open grate. When he recovered a little I got him to help me lift her on to the bed. There was some blood from the wound in her head – not a lot, and there were no other signs of injury. All the same it was obvious that she was dead. I did my best to revive her but there was no hope.'

Wycliffe said, 'You were quite sure of that?'

'Quite sure. I trained and worked as a nurse before I went into the antiques business. Julia was dead, there's no doubt of that.'

Clare Jordan was pale and her hands were clenched. She had the gift of graphic narrative and while she was talking, for Wycliffe at least, the little interview room had become that bedroom at Kellycoryk.

There was an interval and he said, 'Would you like to take a break? A cup of tea or something?'

She shook her head. 'No, I'm going through with this.'

Lucy Lane asked, 'Did you see or hear anything of Crispin during all this?'

'Nothing. But that is not so surprising as it sounds. Crispin had the little room right at the east end which is still his, while the bedroom Roger shared with Julia was more than halfway along the corridor. In any case these quarrels between Roger and Julia, though they could be violent, were never very noisy.'

'All right. Will you tell us what happened next?'

Clare Jordan took a handkerchief from her bag and patted her lips. 'I assumed that we would call a doctor at once but Roger pleaded with me, begged me, to wait until morning.'

'Did he give any reason?'

'He said that he wanted to be alone with his wife, to pray at her bedside. Roger has always been a puzzle to me. In some respects he seems to have a faith that is simple and childlike. Yet sometimes I have the impression that his religion is no more than a kind of superstition.'

Lucy Lane said, 'Anyway, you left him alone, as he wished.'

'Yes. I went back to my own room.'

'And?'

'For a long time I lay in bed, listening, and heard nothing. Then, I hardly know how to explain or excuse it, I fell asleep ... In circumstances that I would not have believed it possible to sleep, I slept ... Whether it would have made any difference if I'd stayed awake, I don't know.'

Lucy Lane said, 'And when you did wake?'

'When I woke it was getting light. I got out of bed and went to the other room. There was no sign of Roger nor of the body. The bed was as I had last seen it, tumbled, and with a blood-stained pillow case, but apart from that there was nothing to show what had happened.' She broke off abruptly, and said with a helpless little gesture, 'I think, after all, I would like that cup of tea.'

Lucy Lane spoke for the tape, 'This interview is suspended at 11.24.' And she switched off the recorder.

On the other side of the wall the other interview had reached a similar point. Kersey said, 'All right, you admit removing your wife's body, but the question is, why did you do it?'

Roger sat, staring at the table top. When it seemed that he would not answer he ran a hand through his short, greying curls and, without looking up, said, 'My main reason was that I'm a coward. If I had let things take their course, when it came out that Julia was pregnant by another man, I would have been accused of murder, at least of manslaughter . . . I couldn't face it. Even if I was acquitted I wouldn't have wanted to go on living . . .'

Another interval before he added, 'I did not kill my wife. I did *not*! She slipped down as though she had fainted, and struck her head as she fell.'

'You said your main reason – there were others?'

The question seemed to trouble him even more deeply than the others. He played a little tattoo on the table top with his fingers. 'I am what I am, I can't help it. To me, Julia was a Kemp – only by marriage, it is true, but still a Kemp, and I wanted her in some private place where I could pray for her soul, especially in some place where that man, whoever he may be, could not approach her.'

'You have no idea who he was?'

'None and I don't wish to know.'

When the interview was resumed next door, and after the ritual announcement for the tape, Wycliffe said, 'You were about to tell us what happened on the morning after Julia's death.'

'Yes. It was about half-past four when I returned to the bedroom and found it empty. I was frantic, I couldn't imagine what had happened.

'Then, perhaps half an hour later, Roger turned up. It was strange, uncanny. I had never seen him so calm. He said, "I've laid Julia to rest." And that was all I could get from him at first. I pointed out that he would have to tell somebody exactly what had happened, that there would be an inquiry, an inquest . . . But all he would say was, "Julia is at rest; she will never be seen again on this earth and I shall pray for her soul."

'I lost my temper but it got me nowhere. It was a nightmare.' She stopped speaking and seemed to be reliving those moments.

'Then, as though he were planning something ordinary and rational, he explained what he intended that we should do. Of course it was the boat trip, the accident, and all that followed . . .' Her voice trailed off.

'And how did you react?'

'I was horrified. It seemed inconceivable.'

'But you agreed.'

She nodded. 'In the end, yes. He said that if I didn't he would certainly be charged with murder . . . He went on about the disgrace, the scandal that would destroy the family. He even said that I owed it to the family after being brought up by them. I don't know how long we kept it up but at the finish I decided that in view of what he'd already done, to do as he wanted would be the lesser of two evils. After all, Julia was dead and nothing would bring her back . . .'

'Did you then, or at any time since until now, find out what he had done with his wife's body?'

She shivered. 'No! And I have never wanted to know.'

'Just one more question: Did you know that Julia Kemp was pregnant?'

A shrewd look. 'I guessed as much.'

'Was it ever mentioned between you?'

'No.'

'Had you any idea as to who the father might be?'

She hesitated, lips pursed. 'I had a suspicion that there was something between Julia and Roger's brother, Francis. But that was all it was – a suspicion.'

It was sometime later when Roger Kemp and Clare Jordan left the police station, having initialled their tapes. No charges were brought, but it was made clear that the investigation would continue.

Back at the Incident Room with Kersey and Lucy Lane, Wycliffe telephoned John Harvey at his surgery. 'I think we should talk; this afternoon if possible.'

Harvey sounded anxious. 'At your Incident Room?'

Wycliffe hesitated, he wanted the contact to be unofficial. 'I would prefer your cottage.'

Wycliffe lunched at the New Inn with Lucy Lane and Kersey. Mrs Sara gave them a small room to themselves at the back of the house.

'A bit more private, like.' She went on in the same breath, 'Today it's a fricassee of chicken, and a nice light almond sponge-pudding to follow with cream or custard . . .'

When they were served Kersey put down his bait. 'So the first Mrs Kemp had a heart attack during a fairly athletic quarrel with her husband. She fell, hit her head on the fender, and it was all over.' He paused to masticate the latest forkful. 'I suppose it could happen.'

Wycliffe refused to be drawn. After lunch he walked down through the village and along the cliff road to the cove. The sky was uniformly overcast with high cloud, colours were muted, and not a breath of air disturbed the glassy sea. Wycliffe found the brooding stillness oppressive.

No sign of Helen or of any life in the cove, but Harvey's Deux-Chevaux was parked by his cottage and Harvey met him at the door.

'This is building up for a storm.'

They sat by the open door. Wycliffe was facing Julia's painting of the cove and Kellycoryk seen from the sea. Magical and sinister; they were the words which had come to his mind when he first saw the painting and they came back to him now. Harvey, looking tired and haggard, watched him, waiting for him to begin.

'First, I'm sorry that it fell to you to identify your sister; sorry too, for all the circumstances.'

Harvey was silent for a while, then he said, 'It's hard to realize that the boating accident, an event which one has accepted and lived with for several years, turns out to have been no more than a piece of fiction – a charade.' He sounded bitter.

Wycliffe did not rush his fences, he allowed time for the silences to work. Then, 'I'm wondering whether Franks has mentioned his findings to you?'

'No, Franks was strictly professional and I was, quite properly, treated like any other relative. You've had his report?'

Wycliffe gave him the substance of what Franks had said and Harvey listened until he had finished.

'So Julia was pregnant.'

'You had no suspicion?'

'None. She didn't tell me and I wasn't seeing enough of her to tumble to it for myself.' There was another break before he went on, 'This blow to the head – there's no indication of how it came about?'

'Before I answer that question, do you know anything of your sister's medical history? Did she, for example, suffer from hypertension or a heart condition? Was she subject to fits . . . ?'

Harvey looked at him in surprise. 'She never confided in me

as a doctor. When she needed one she went to Tim Paul in St Mawes.' Wycliffe thought that he had finished but after a time he went on, 'Tim did mention to me once, in confidence, that there was evidence to suggest a degree of mitral stenosis and that he had recommended her to see a cardiologist but she had flatly refused. Tim assured me that he would monitor the situation and that he wasn't unduly concerned.' Harvey broke off abruptly. 'Why are you asking me this?'

Wycliffe said, 'Franks thinks that your sister might have struck her head in falling and the question arises how she came to fall.'

Harvey nodded and Wycliffe continued, 'From what you know of her medical condition, does that strike you as credible?'

Harvey hesitated. 'If, as you say, she was four months pregnant, having had no medical supervision, and given her heart condition, I have to say that it does.'

Chapter Ten

Thursday evening/Friday morning 13/14 May

'Here is a severe weather warning: southwesterly gales are expected to affect Cornwall and south Devon in the early hours of tomorrow morning. Winds are likely to reach storm force on exposed coasts and, in rain squalls, gusts may exceed ninety miles per hour with the possibility of structural damage. Gales with heavy rain will continue into the daylight hours and winds will remain strong until at least midday.'

Agnes always paid attention to the weather forecast and this one was the signal for a strategic placing of buckets in attics and roof spaces. She was not deterred by the stillness of the evening.

The Kemps, all four of them, ate their evening meal with scarcely a word exchanged and Roger did not refer to his interview with the police. When the meal was over he turned to Agnes and said, 'I'm expecting a visitor, so if you hear voices . . .'

'Doesn't this visitor have a name?'

Roger looked at her, his expression totally blank, and said nothing.

At about half-past ten Agnes went to bed.

The weather was still quiet but at a little after midnight the wind began to pick up and within an hour it was roaring around the old house, punctuated by explosive gusts and violent rain squalls which seemed to threaten the windows if not the walls themselves.

As usual Agnes's alarm clock went off at seven but she was already up. The wind was unabated and outside pandemonium reigned. Inside, windows rattled and from time to time the whole building seemed to shudder. She had discovered without surprise that the electricity was off.

Still in her dressing gown, she had made a quick check on her buckets and bowls: two fresh leaks, though nothing calamitous. Now, washed and dressed, she was in her kitchen, thanking God for the Aga.

At sometime after eight she knocked on the library door. 'Breakfast, Roger!'

There was no response, but that was not unusual. When she returned to the kitchen Crispin was already in his place. His right hand was bandaged and blood had seeped through to stain the dressing.

A strange look passed between them. Complicity? 'How does it feel?'

'All right.'

'Not throbbing?'

'No.'

Roger did not come, and after ten or fifteen minutes Agnes went back to the library. In the hall she glanced up the stairs and saw Isobel in her dressing gown, apparently half-asleep, on her way to their only bathroom.

Agnes called to her, 'I'm trying to get your father in to breakfast.'

The Wycliffes, awakened in the small hours, were having their first experience of the front line during a real blow. When they finally convinced themselves that their cottage, having been there for a hundred and fifty years, would probably survive the night, they went back to bed and, improbable as it seemed, they slept.

It was broad daylight, or as near to it as conditions allowed, when Wycliffe drew back the curtains in the living room and looked out through a deposit of finest salt crystals on a grey waste of sea streaked with white. He had already discovered that there was no electricity. Out of curiosity he tried the telephone; it too, was off, but there was an RT in his car outside.

The pendulum wall clock struck eight on its tinny gong. He was late – very. So what? It was strange, though he had noticed before that the violence of nature, a gale, a thunderstorm, seemed to put him on a high, and to trivialize the concerns of everyday. 'What is man that thou art mindful of him?' And all that.

So he searched for a little Gaz stove that he remembered seeing in one of the cupboards and set about brewing coffee. Then, with a sense of achievement, he offered the result at the bedside of his wife.

The house felt cold, and he kindled a fire in the open grate. Driftwood, which they had collected at a whim, came into its own and by the time Helen was down the place was almost cosy. She set about getting breakfast on the little stove.

It was only then that his thoughts returned to the case and to wondering where events were leading. The death of the first Mrs Kemp was unlikely to result in a charge more serious than conspiracy. Conviction on a conspiracy charge could mean anything from a suspended sentence to a long term of imprisonment but his gut feeling was that the scales would be weighted in favour of leniency. The shooting of Bridget Kemp was a very different matter; the only feasible charge was murder, but such a charge must be supported by evidence and so far there was none that would get past the CPS let alone the courts.

His broodings were interrupted by the sound of a car engine which was cut, followed by knocking on the front door.

Wycliffe opened the door to a miniature tornado of wind. John Harvey pale and agitated was on the doorstep. 'I'm sorry to burst in on you like this but I had to – the phone isn't working. I've just come from Kellycoryk . . . Roger has shot himself.'

'He's dead?'

'Yes. Crispin came over for me. I've got my car outside.'

Wycliffe said, 'We'll get over there as soon as I've been in touch with my people on the RT.'

'Wouldn't it be better if I went back there right away?'

Wycliffe had to spell it out. 'I'm sorry, but you would be putting yourself and me in an invidious position. We will stay together.'

It was obvious that Harvey was shaken by the implication.

A few minutes later they were out in the grey turbulent world. The rain had stopped, but the wind was carrying salt spray well inland. The stream had overflowed its banks but as far as he could see, the road and the bridge were clear.

To his relief he was able to speak to the Incident Room. Kersey was already there.

Wycliffe gave him the news. 'I want you to stay there for the moment; see that the coroner is notified, also SOCO and

Forensic. I'll talk to Franks. We need a small team. Is Lucy with you . . . ? Then send her along. I think we have to look at this with an open mind.'

Harvey, sheltering in the car at his side and still coming to terms with his implied status, said, 'You're treating this as a suspicious death?'

'As you know, I haven't even seen him, but I can't afford to be wrong.'

A moment or two later they were in the drive on the way to the house. Twigs and small branches torn from the shrubs littered the track and were crunched under the car wheels. A fresh rain squall battered the car from the rear and, in front of the house, Wycliffe pulled in as close as he could to the steps. He got out, put his finger on the doorbell, and kept it there.

John Harvey joined him. 'I left them in the kitchen. It's the only room that's warm in the place and with no electricity you can hardly see to think.'

It was Agnes who answered the bell. She was white-faced but composed. They had to help her close the door against the force of the wind.

Wycliffe spoke to her sympathetically, but she merely said, 'You know where to go.'

Wycliffe turned to Harvey. 'All right, let's take a look and you can tell me what you know.'

He led the way down the short passage to the library and opened the door. As he did so he received a shock. Roger was seated at his table, leaning back in his chair in almost exactly the posture in which Wycliffe had found him two days earlier. As then, his eyes were wide open and they seemed to stare at the ceiling, though now the expression in those eyes was one of astonishment. And there was another difference: there was a small, neat entrance hole in his right temple. Wycliffe looked for an exit wound but there was none. Two thin trickles of blood had run down his right cheek and one had dripped on to the lapel of his jacket.

Wycliffe moved around the table. Kemp's arms hung straight down, and on the worn carpet not far from the fingers of his right hand there was a little pistol with an ivory butt.

'Who found him?'

Harvey seemed lost in his own thoughts. 'What . . . ? Oh, it wasn't quite like that. It seems that this morning, as usual, Agnes banged on the library door and told him that his breakfast was ready. He didn't answer, but he never does. When, after a little while, he didn't turn up she went back to the library and it was then that she found the door was locked. She called to him but got no reply. She then tried the door which opens from the back hall into the little room adjoining the library but that too was locked.

'In the end, Crispin went outside and saw his father through the window. He smashed a pane of glass and cut his hand doing it but he reached the catch and raised the sash. Of course he climbed in. The phone wasn't working so Agnes sent him to fetch me.'

The two sash-windows had small panes, and one of the panes, near the catch in the left-hand window, had been smashed, leaving a jagged hole through which rain now blew into the room.

Wycliffe turned his attention to the desk; the usual litter of books and papers, but immediately in front of Roger was a clean sheet of paper on which a message had been written in block capitals: 'THIS IS ONLY WHAT I DESERVED.' A felt-tipped pen lay beside the paper.

'Did the boy tell you exactly what had happened?'

'No. He said that his father had been taken ill and would I come over at once. He was obviously in shock and I didn't question him. It was only when I got here that I heard the full story from Agnes.'

'Presumably you made some sort of examination to confirm that life was extinct. How long, in your opinion, has he been dead?'

Harvey ran his fingers through his hair. 'Of course I was expecting to be asked that and I've thought about it. Rigor is by no means complete but, as I judge it without disturbing him, the body has not yet reached room temperature. In my opinion he's been there a good part of the night. I'd say sometime in the small hours.'

'Nobody's mentioned hearing anything that could have been a shot?'

'No.'

'By the way, what's happened to the cat?'

'The cat? I've no idea.'

'It wasn't here when you arrived with the boy?'

Harvey looked puzzled. 'No, is it important?' Then understanding dawned, and he seemed surprised at Wycliffe's interest. 'Oh, the Kemp moggies!'

Wycliffe did not reply, he was preoccupied, and his manner was abrupt. 'I'm going to take a look around. I'm not entirely satisfied that this is suicide. Perhaps you will join the family.'

Harvey looked doubtful but he said, 'Of course.'

Wycliffe went on, 'Obviously they will be distressed but we shall need to talk to them later.'

Left alone, Wycliffe stood for a minute or two looking down at the dead man. He could not shake off a feeling of unreality. It was corny; a 1930's thriller with the squire shot at his desk in a locked library. Wycliffe recalled a cavalcade of fictional, homicidal butlers.

And yet there was nothing inherently unlikely in what seemed to have happened. It would not be surprising if Roger had become suicidal. And if he had decided to kill himself he might well have chosen to do so in the place where he spent most of his waking hours. It might even be expected that he would lock the doors for fear of being disturbed during those agonizing moments when his resolve was faced with the ultimate test . . . All the same . . .

All very reasonable but Wycliffe did not believe a word of it. And at bottom he felt guilty; he had hesitated about what line to take with Roger. There had been enough circumstantial evidence to detain him for further questioning in connection with the death of his second wife. Kersey, left to himself, would certainly have done so and Roger might now still be alive.

From his car he phoned Franks and spoke to the pathologist's secretary.

'He's due in at any minute, Mr Wycliffe. I'll get him to contact you . . .'

Back in the library he was startled momentarily by a flicker, then the lamp on Roger's table lit up, its circle of light achieving a bizarre effect: the table top with its papers and Roger's torso, brightly lit but leaving the head in shadow.

The power was back on. He searched for and found a bank of switches which he flicked over. Half a dozen ceiling lights came alive; they were low-powered and grimy, but even so there was a dramatic transformation. The room with its elegant proportions, the towering bookcases with their orderly rows of dimly lit spines, the tall windows with their red velvet curtains, were replaced by peeling, cracked plaster, ubiquitous dust, a littered floor, and faded, threadbare hangings.

He had seen enough of suicides with a handgun to beware of attaching too much significance to the posture of the victim and to whether or not the weapon was retained in the hand that fired it. All the same, he had never before come across a suicide lolling back in his chair, staring at the ceiling.

Thoughtful, he moved about, looking at this and that but disturbing nothing. He came to the door which led, presumably, into the little room where Roger spent some of his nights. The door was partly open and he pushed it wide. A heavy curtain drawn across the window excluded most of what light there was. He felt for, and found, a light switch.

The room was little more than a passage. A massive settee took up most of the space and on it was a grubby pillow with a couple of carriage rugs. The only other furniture was a kitchen chair and an electric fire with fireclay elements which should have been in the Science Museum. The floorboards were uncovered except for a thin mat beside the settee.

Another door at the far end of the little room was locked but there was a key in the lock. Wycliffe opened the door and found himself in a small, tiled hall with a passage leading off, presumably to the kitchen area. There was also a glass-panelled door to the outside. The key of this door too was in the lock and it opened into the alleyway between the house and the ruins.

Wycliffe stepped out into the alleyway. It was not raining but wind still whistled and roared around the building. A little to his right was the window of the passage room from which he had just come, the room where Roger had spent most of his nights recently. On the night that Bridget Kemp disappeared, her car must have stood outside that window for more than an hour. Above his head were two more windows, not far apart, one belonging to Isobel's room, the other to Crispin's. It was from one of those that Crispin claimed to have seen the car being driven away – by, as he said, a woman.

As Wycliffe returned to the library he was again troubled by the posture of the dead man, so reminiscent of how he had seen the man alive a couple of days earlier. Of course it was just possible that he had shot himself or even been shot while in that position, but Wycliffe was uneasy. He went closer, and now, with the lights on, he noticed something which had escaped him before; the top sheet of a little pile of manuscript on the table carried two spots of blood but they meant nothing to him at the time.

He was interrupted by the ringing of the doorbell and went to answer it himself.

Odd. A few days earlier Kellycoryk had been inaccessible, an intriguingly mysterious house and a family on the fringe of history which he could only read about. Now, here he was, on the inside, only to discover that the house was no more than a shell inhabited by the sad remnants of a family that had lost its way.

Lucy Lane and WPC Rees were waiting on the doorstep. There was a message to telephone Franks at his office, so he left the newcomers in the hall while he went outside to his car phone.

Franks said, 'Kersey told me that Kemp has shot himself.'

'That is what I want to be sure of.'

'It must go a long way towards solving your problems, Charles. Surely, you don't want me?'

'I'm afraid I do.'

They needed a room in the house which they could use as a base. No point in involving Agnes, so Wycliffe tried the door across the hall from the library. The room was large, and still impressive, but entirely devoid of furniture. He tried the room behind, and fared better; it was the dining room, still with its gate-table and a set of chairs, but little else. A bloom of mould dulled every polished surface. It was there that he briefed his troops, including Kersey who had just joined them.

Wycliffe began with a review of the situation as he now saw it and went on, 'We must officially notify Roger's brother, Francis, and his cousin Clare Jordan. Perhaps you will see to that right away, Lucy. Later we shall want statements from all concerned. Clare Jordan and Kemp himself were at the nick until three in the afternoon yesterday when they were released without charge pending further inquiries. So watch your step in dealing with the Jordan woman or we may be tripped up by lawyers.

'Leave Agnes until I've had a chat with her. Reports and queries to Mr Kersey.'

He found Agnes alone in the kitchen, sitting at the big table, a teapot, a carton of milk and a mug in front of her, but there was a strong smell of spirits and her cheeks were lightly flushed. Not surprising in the circumstances but the bottle was hidden. He offered sympathy. 'I'll trouble you as little as possible.'

She looked at him without speaking. How old was Agnes? As far as he could remember she must be still short of fifty, yet in her appearance and attitudes she could have passed for the middle sixties.

'Has Dr Harvey left?'

'He had surgery and I told him there was no point in him hanging around here.'

'How about Isobel and Crispin?'

A slight shrug. 'They're probably up in their rooms. They never tell me where they're going.'

'Are they very upset?'

She grimaced. 'How would I know? There's no way of telling. Nobody says what they mean in this house, let alone what they feel. It's probably hit Crispy, but I wouldn't like to say about his sister.'

It sounded reasonable yet there was something which made him wary.

Agnes said, 'Do you want a cup of tea? It's not long made.'

He pulled out a chair and sat down. 'Thank you. I'd like one.'

She fetched a mug from a cupboard. 'Help yourself.' Her movements were listless, jerky and uncertain.

'Do you feel up to telling me exactly what happened this morning?'

She told her story and it squared with the account he had had from Harvey. 'Just one point, was the cat in the library when Crispin broke in?'

She paused briefly, 'No, he wasn't. I've never thought of it until now . . . Odd that; always where you found Roger, you found the cat. And I haven't seen him since, either.'

Wycliffe said, 'Strange creatures!' and changed the subject. 'When did you last see your brother?'

'Last night when we had our meal – if you can call it that.'

'Did he mention what had happened at the police station?'

'Not a word.'

'And after the meal?'

'He went back to his books as usual. He said he was expecting a visitor.'

'Did he tell you who he was expecting?'

'No, but there was somebody. I happened to be outside the library at about ten and I heard him talking. I didn't hear whoever was with him.'

So Agnes had been eavesdropping, or trying to.

'Have you any idea who it was?'

'No idea.'

Didn't know or wouldn't say?

'And at no time during the evening or night did you hear a shot or a noise which could have been one?'

'No, but that's not surprising, there was enough noise from the wind. I thought the roof might come off.' She sipped her tea, watching him over the rim of her cup, and when she spoke again it was in a different, reminiscent vein. She said, 'A fortnight a year.'

He waited, and she went on, 'A fortnight a year was all the holiday I ever had from this place. I used to go to Torquay to stay with a girl I went to school with.' She put her cup down before continuing. 'Mavis Tate. She emigrated to Australia a couple of years back, so now I never leave this place.'

He sensed that she needed no prompting, that he would get more by listening. Agnes probably suffered from having no one who would listen.

'And my fortnight away, five years ago, was what started it all. If I hadn't gone away . . .' She made a movement of impatience. 'They were like children! Not safe to be left on their own.'

'You are speaking of your brother and his first wife?'

She did not bother to answer that. 'I mean, they should never have married. Julia's temper was liable to flare up without warning, and Roger exasperated her . . . God knows he would exasperate a saint.'

'They quarrelled a lot?'

She finished her tea and patted her lips with a grubby handkerchief. 'No, it didn't happen often, but when it did she could become hysterical . . . Violent sometimes. Roger had no idea of how to cope with her and that was when they needed me.' She stopped speaking for a moment or two before adding: 'And that last time . . . Well, I wasn't there.'

Wycliffe still did not speak; he felt sure that there was more to come.

Agnes raised her eyes to meet his. 'But whatever your post-mortem shows I don't believe that he killed her.'

Wycliffe allowed the silence to develop before breaking it with a remark that sounded almost casual. 'You've known all along that the boating accident was a fable.'

She did not answer at once, then, 'I suspected something but I didn't know the truth.' She made a gesture of impatience. 'I didn't want to know!'

'You had no idea that her body was concealed in Mayne's Closet?'

'No, I did not. That was a shock.'

Wycliffe handed her a print of one of Fox's photographs, taken in Mayne's Closet before the chest was disturbed. It showed the statue of the Virgin and the brass candlesticks with their candles in place. The inscription on the slate top was clearly readable.

Agnes studied the photograph. 'I can understand this; it doesn't really surprise me. It was as near as he could get to giving her a Christian burial.'

'You see that the date of her death is given as the thirteenth – the day before the supposed boating accident?'

She nodded. 'Yes. That doesn't surprise me either. Julia obviously died on the thirteenth and Roger could never have brought himself to lie to the Virgin.'

The way in which she said this was almost contemptuous.

For a little longer they sat in silence while the wind roared around the house. In the end it was again Wycliffe who spoke first. 'Your brother went to incredible lengths to cover up the way in which his first wife died.'

Agnes gave a small shrug. 'That was Roger; he could never face reality.'

'And his second wife? Do you think he might have tried something similar there?'

Agnes made an irritable movement. 'That is nonsense! What

could he have done? In any case I've told you all I know about that, and Roger is dead.'

'I gather that relations between your brother and his second wife were quite different from those he had had with his first.'

She made an emphatic gesture. 'There was no comparison! He married that woman only because he thought she would help him to keep this place.' Agnes glanced around the barn-like kitchen and her expression was derisive.

Wycliffe persisted. 'Are you satisfied that your brother took his own life?'

She looked up sharply, then began fiddling with the frayed edge of the tablecloth. 'Who on earth do you think would want to kill him?' She stood up and reached across the table for his mug, dismissive. 'Anyway, you're the policeman.'

It was five minutes to eleven by the kitchen clock but to Wycliffe it seemed an age since he had made coffee on a Gaz stove in the cottage.

When Wycliffe left the kitchen he found Isobel waiting for him in the passage. She said, 'They've got Crispin in there now; I must talk to you before it's my turn.' Her manner was tense and urgent.

He followed her to the front hall and to a door beneath the stairs which looked like the door of a cupboard but actually opened into a little room where there was a window high in the wall. In the dimly lit hall he had not seen her clearly but here, where the light was better, he saw the dark-ringed eyes, the pale, drawn features, and was touched.

The room was furnished with a table and several kitchen chairs, one upside down on the other; books, looking like discards from a second-hand shop, were piled on the floor around the walls. And everywhere there was dust.

Isobel placed a couple of chairs and waited for him to sit down before launching into what she had to say. She looked straight into his eyes, holding his gaze. 'You won't understand, but I want you to know that I hate this place; I've grown up hating it, and the way we live . . . Our lives have always been dominated by Father's obsession. We are not like other people — we can't *mix*!'

Wycliffe said, 'But surely, you're of age, you've got a job, you could have broken away.'

She made an expressive little gesture of frustration. 'Don't you think I've thought of that? But wherever I've been, wherever I go, I'm always "the Kemp girl". I stand out; I don't know how to behave!'

There was more of the same and though she spoke with vigour she paused now and then to choose her words. It was as if she were being driven to a commitment that she was scared of making.

Wycliffe sat motionless, wearing that cow-like expression which exasperated his wife but had served him well in the job.

Isobel relaxed and her manner became more reflective. 'Of course Crispy has always been different, he's never felt as I do.'

A long pause, then, 'While Mother was alive it was bearable, but when she died . . . I missed her desperately and, I know it sounds absurd, I also felt let down by her death – like a victim. And I suppose I became spiteful, I wanted somebody to blame and, of course, Father was the obvious one. He seemed to have been the cause of it all . . .'

Another long pause before she went on, 'But I never really believed the things I hinted about him.' There were tears in her eyes and in her voice; she turned away to hide her emotion.

Wycliffe waited, but no more came and in the end he said, 'I don't think you've told me all that you intended to say.'

She raised her eyes to meet his and spoke with a certain doggedness. 'I just want you to know that Father isn't – wasn't – a bad man. His trouble was that he could never face up to things. He dreaded change, or anything that forced him to look outside this place. He was like an ostrich . . . He couldn't face losing Kellycoryk and he couldn't face the changes that might have made it possible to keep it.'

She brought her pale hands together on the table top and stared down at them. 'Things that have happened recently have made me understand him better. I think I can understand now why he did what he did about Mother. He just couldn't face the suspicion, the questions, the meddling in his life that he would have had to put up with if they knew Mother had died in the middle of one of their quarrels.'

There was a break in her voice as she added, 'So, in a sort of charade, he hid her body, then made a little shrine out of the hiding place.' One might have thought she was speaking about the capricious behaviour of a child.

Wycliffe gave her time then, very quietly, he said, 'So you have never really believed that your father was responsible for the deaths of either your mother or your stepmother?'

Her response was emphatic and immediate. 'No!'

'And did he take his own life?'

She straightened up, facing him, worried, her manner less assured. She shook her head. 'All I can say is, I don't think so; I can't believe that he did. But who . . . ?' Her voice let her down.

Wycliffe was gentle. 'Thank you for talking to me. I'm afraid you will still be asked to make a statement about the events of last night but perhaps you will clear up one or two points for me now.'

She waited like a well-behaved schoolgirl.

'Apart from the noise of the storm, you heard nothing unusual in the night?'

'Nothing.'

'Nothing that might have been a shot?'

'No.'

'And what was the first thing you saw or heard this morning about what had happened?'

She stopped to think. 'I was on my way to the bathroom; Agnes was down in the hall and she called up something about trying to get Father in to breakfast. I didn't take much notice.'

'And after that?'

'When I came downstairs Agnes had decided there was something wrong and Crispy had broken a pane of glass in one of the library windows to get in.' She spoke with a curious detachment which puzzled him.

Crispin was being interviewed in the dining room by Kersey and Lanyon. Hollow-eyed and tense but lucid, he gave his account of the finding of his father's body, of breaking into the library, and of fetching Dr Harvey. He spoke slowly, with occasional breaks, but remained coherent and concise.

Kersey said, 'When you broke into the library the main door

and the door from the passage room into the back hall were both locked. Is that correct?'

'Yes.'

'Were the keys in the locks?'

'Yes.'

'So, in your opinion, your father locked himself in the library and shot himself – is that what you think?'

'It seems that he must have done.'

'You are prepared to accept that as what actually happened?'

'Yes.'

'In your earlier evidence you said that you thought it was a woman who drove your stepmother's car away from Kellycoryk on the night she was killed. Do you still hold to that?'

'No, it was my father. I saw him.'

'You lied in order to protect him?'

The boy hesitated. 'I suppose so.'

Kersey said, 'You've hurt your hand.'

Crispin looked down at his bandaged hand. 'Yes. I cut it against the broken glass in trying to reach the window catch.'

Chapter Eleven

Friday late morning (continued)

Wycliffe let himself out of the house by the back door into the aftermath of the storm. The wind still blew but it was losing heart and there were even intervals of calm. Overhead the sky was still threatening but the rain had stopped. All that remained to mark the passage of the storm were battered shrubs, a few branches torn from the trees, and the swollen stream.

With no specific purpose in mind he wanted to renew contact with Chylathva, with Francis, and with Molly. Laughable as it seemed, even to him, he had come to think of that couple as representing some sort of norm, a species of yardstick against which he could measure the events in the big house.

As he walked he brooded on Roger Kemp; according to Miss Scott's little book, he was probably the forty-ninth Kemp to succeed to the tenure of Kellycoryk. A strange man! Wycliffe regretted that he lacked the facility to produce thumbnail character sketches of fellow human beings. He had to make his approach through vague approximations, odd phrases that occurred to him. A strange man ... A semi-recluse, obsessed by his inheritance and his ancestry ... A man who, lacking any apparent sense of pride, was burdened with an almost neurotic awareness of responsibility ... A timid man – No! That wasn't right; no timid man could have done what he had done to cover up the death of his first wife ... A fearful man – fearful of anything that threatened the continuity of life at Kellycoryk; that was better. But a man possessed of a certain courage ... Above all, perhaps, a foolish man, who consistently refused to read the writing on the wall; a man ready to use all his energies and ingenuity to hold back the future ...

A murderer? If Roger Kemp had ended up by killing himself

with that little ivory-handled pistol then there could be little doubt that he had murdered his wife.

But Wycliffe shook his head as he walked, in total rejection of the idea.

Scarcely noticing what he was about he had negotiated a number of fresh obstacles in the path, mainly fallen branches, but in a couple of places the bank of the stream and the path itself had been washed away so that he had to pick his way around an expanse of black, glutinous mud.

However, Chylathva, when he reached it, looked the same as ever. There was no car outside, so one of the pair was probably away. But the front door was open as usual. He scraped and scuffed mud from his shoes as best he could and while he was at it Molly appeared, puffy eyed, looking as though she had just woken from sleep. She yawned and stretched without embarrassment. 'I must have dropped off. Francis is out. I haven't seen him since this morning. When he heard about Roger he pushed off.

'A couple of your lot came here looking for him about an hour ago. It's anybody's guess when he turns up now, and in what sort of state he'll be.' She added after a pause, 'I suppose it was him you came to see?'

Wycliffe hardly knew himself but as she moved away from the door he followed her into the living room.

'How did you and Francis hear the news? Who told you?'

'Crispin. It was this morning sometime, I'm not sure when. That boy's in a bad way; at the end of his tether. If somebody doesn't take him in hand soon he'll do away with himself.'

Wycliffe sat in a rickety Windsor chair. The heat from a blazing wood fire disposed of any chill from the open door and he felt strangely at peace. The barn-like room with its wainscotted granite walls, open fireplace, sisal mats and basic furniture appealed to him. If the pathos of Francis's nudes disturbed him, there was no need to look that way.

And Molly, warm, loose and unshockable, went with it. Here there were no taboos, no pretences. Or so it seemed. In his present mood he could find it in his heart to envy Francis. But there must be a fly in Francis's ointment somewhere; the one that drove him to drink.

Molly said, 'They think Roger shot himself – is that right?'

'That's what it looked like.'

'You may as well know – he would tell you himself if he was here – Francis went to see Roger last night. Roger asked him to come.'

'What about?'

Molly reached for a packet of cigarettes from the table, lit one and drew on it like an addict. 'His lordship hasn't confided in me.'

Something in her manner convinced him that she was holding back. He said, 'I think you've got some idea. When did he go and when did he come back?'

She looked at him through the veil of cigarette smoke. 'You're pushing it a bit. Shouldn't you ask *him*? Anyway, I'm sure he'd tell you himself. He left about nine and he was back just after eleven. It was too rough to walk down through that bloody jungle so, as it was my night off from the pub, he took the car.'

Wycliffe was in a mood to listen rather than question so he said nothing and Molly was left to fill the silence. After a little while she said, 'He and his brother were a lot closer than you might think, and whatever Roger had to say to him last night, went deep. When he got back it was obvious that he'd had a shock.'

She smoked for a while, reflective; then, 'The Kemps are a funny lot; the three of them, Agnes, Roger and Francis . . . I get the impression that they never had parents like most people, they're more like if they'd been brought up in an institution . . . Anyway, this morning, when he heard that Roger was dead it pushed him over the top.'

'Did he say anything?'

'Not much. When Crispin told him Roger had shot himself, he became angry and shouted at Crispin as though it was the boy's fault, then he said, "This is bloody impossible!" I told him to calm down and he said, "I've got to think about this," and pushed off. I hope that doesn't mean what I think it does.'

Wycliffe, on his feet, wandered over to the famous picture which was almost a mural. As he got closer, so the composition and even the figures were lost in swathes and flurries of colour, like feathers on some exotic bird; the paint was almost structural, laid on with a palette knife – impasto.

For an instant he saw Isobel's pale face, intense and

half-fearful. '. . . She was always referring to "Pasto" as she called him. I suppose it was her pet name for the man.'

It made sense; they were both painters and Julia had probably teased him about his lavish use of paint. She was a Gwen John painter.

Molly said, 'That sounds like him now.'

A moment or two later Francis's old banger pulled up outside the window and Francis came in; a leaner, older, grimmer Francis; or so it seemed. Even the Kemp features had become more pronounced. It was not the first time that Wycliffe had seen how stress can age people in a few days, and how those changes can be as promptly reversed when the tension is removed.

'Ah, the top brass!' Francis was worried, the banter was routine. 'I was thinking about coming to see you.' He pulled out a chair and sat astride it, arms resting on the back. He glanced across at Molly who was putting fresh wood on the fire. 'I expect she told you that last evening Roger phoned me – he asked me to come and see him at nine in his library. He said the side door would be unlocked so that I could get in without disturbing the others . . . Of course I went.'

He was staring at Wycliffe with his dark, brooding eyes and he seemed to find difficulty in deciding how to go on. He made a curious gesture with his hands, raising them from the chairback and letting them drop. 'I don't know whether I should be telling you this; I promised Rog I would leave the decision to him but now that he's gone . . .'

Suddenly Wycliffe saw in Francis a reflection of his brother; the same tendency to convoluted and ponderous reasoning, the same irrational hesitations and reservations, the same lack of judgement which had brought Roger to disaster. Now, imposed on all that was the slightly absurd image of Pasto, the secret lover.

He was irritated; he had had enough of the Kemps. When he spoke his manner was incisive, almost brutal. 'You were going to tell me that your brother did not kill his wife but that it was he who drove her car with her body in it to the headland, and that it was he who put her body into the sea . . . is that it?'

Francis looked bemused. 'Yes.'

'In other words it was an attempt at damage limitation of the same sort and of the same level of foolhardiness as the one he carried out five years earlier following the death of his first wife.'

Francis was stung. 'I think you should know that whatever Rog did he did it as much to protect others as himself—'

Wycliffe cut him short. 'But above all to sustain the Kemp myth. I want to make it clear that we have finished with these family charades. I want to know just two things: first, who killed Bridget Kemp, and second, whether your brother killed himself or was murdered? I have my own ideas on both questions but I need evidence, and I intend to get it.'

Molly had paused in the act of tending her fire, seemingly transfixed.

Wycliffe went on, 'If anything your brother told you last night or any other information you may have is relevant, then it is your obvious duty to tell me. And I want that message fully understood by the whole family.'

It took Francis a moment or two to collect his wits. In the end he said, his voice subdued, 'There was nothing. Roger was very careful not to involve anyone else in what he told me.'

Wycliffe stood up. 'Well, I hope that we understand each other better. I have only two more questions: first, did you see anyone other than your brother at Kellycoryk last night?'

'No one.'

'My other question concerns the cat, Coryk. Was he with your brother as usual last night?'

'He was asleep on Roger's work table where he spends most of his time. Why?'

'Coryk seems to have disappeared.'

Wycliffe left Chylathva feeling anything but pleased with himself; his treatment of Francis had served no tactical purpose and might be counter-productive; it had arisen from a sudden impatience with the whole Kemp ethos, with that entangling web of belief and superstition, convention and intrigue, which had scarred the lives of two generations.

On the spur of the moment he decided to take a break, to go back to the cottage and chance whether there would be any lunch. He found fish and chips from the shop in the village, a glass of lager, tea and sympathy.

*   *   *

It was afternoon, the wind had dropped, it no longer rained, and the sun struggled through thinning clouds. Seen from the library the surface of the lake was strewn with the detritus of the storm, while the wilderness of rhododendron and laurel looked as though a great broom had swept over it.

In the middle distance the roofs of the cottages seemed to stand out more starkly and, beyond the cove, the sea was grey, still troubled, still flecked with white.

Franks spent some time examining the body, dictating telegraphic comments to his secretary. Fox, looking like some giant stick-insect, hovered with his camera so that the pathologist's performance was recorded on film.

When Franks turned to Wycliffe he had dropped his usual bantering manner. 'I don't know what to say, Charles. You obviously have your own ideas about this but I can see nothing to suggest that he didn't shoot himself. What I've found in this preliminary is generally consistent with suicide.'

'Don't you see anything unusual in his posture?'

Franks considered. 'I admit that a seated body often slumps forward when shot as this man was, but that really depends on its posture when the shot was fired. This is by no means the first case I've seen where the body has slumped backwards.'

Wycliffe's manner was dogged, almost sullen. 'That body was moved immediately after the shooting; I'm convinced of it. It was moved while blood was still trickling from the wound of entry. There are two little channels on his cheek at an angle to each other, one vertical in respect of its present posture, the other would be vertical if the body was in its original position – slumped over the table. If that doesn't convince you, there are two spots of blood on the top manuscript page of that little heap – just where they would have fallen had he slumped forward.'

Franks was unconvinced. 'It's pretty slim, Charles, but even if he was murdered what would be the point of shifting the body?'

Wycliffe had an opinion about that but not one that he was prepared to argue. He wanted to close the discussion. 'When we have the rhodizinate test on Kemp's hand, if it's positive I'll stop arguing.'

Franks held out. 'But even if it's negative it won't prove that he didn't fire the pistol.'

'No, but it will be a start. What about time of death?'

Franks looked at his watch (a confection mounted in gold which must have been capable of most things short of forecasting the weather). 'I'd say he's been dead for at least twelve, and not more than fifteen hours. That puts it between midnight and three in the morning. I may have more for you when I've had him on the table. Or Forensic may find something to cheer you up. Anyway, as far as I'm concerned, shift him when you want to.'

An hour after Franks had taken himself off, Wycliffe was still in the library. He was not short of company: Fox was there with his assistant, and so were the pair from Forensic – a man and a woman in white overalls looking like acolytes performing some arcane ritual. Wycliffe kept returning to the remains of Roger Kemp and his work table as though loath to tear himself away.

The last message of the dead man: 'This is only what I deserved.' Would a man about to shoot himself really write anything so trite and, at the same time, so objective and detached? Even if he did, why choose to do it in those clumsy block capitals dear to the mentally retarded writer of anonymous letters?

Fox had been working on fingerprints.

'Anything?'

Fox was never guilty of rapid response. After deliberation he said, 'The only prints on the pistol are the dead man's.'

'Anything strike you about them?'

Another interval while the appropriate circuits were engaged then, 'There is only one set, somewhat smeared, as would be made by grasping the weapon with intent to fire.'

'*No* other prints?'

'None, sir.'

'Any explanation?'

Fox considered. 'If Kemp shot himself one would expect to find his prints all over the pistol. I mean, how could it be otherwise?'

'So?'

'It's possible that he was shot by someone else and that the cleaned gun was pressed into his hand to take his prints.' Fox added after a pause, 'Not a very intelligent thing to do.'

For once Wycliffe warmed towards Fox. 'No, I agree. But we
are not dealing with an experienced or a very intelligent killer.'

At a little after four Roger Kemp left his library for the last
time and Wycliffe stood, watching idly, while the two earnest
boffins from Forensic looked as though they might go on indefinitely.

He was mentally adrift, in a mood to grasp at straws. What
he needed was time to think, at least to indulge in that capricious
reverie which he regarded as a substitute for thought.

One of the boffins, the young woman, crouched on the floor,
said, 'There's what looks like fairly fresh blood on the carpet
here.'

She pointed to a patch perhaps the size of a twopenny piece
and to several others that were smaller; they were grouped
together, ten or twelve feet away from Roger's desk, in the
middle of the room.

'How fresh?'

A mild shrug. 'I'd say it's been here ten to twelve hours.'

'You can type it?'

'Hadn't we better decide whether it's human first? These look
like cat hairs on the carpet.'

She was young – twenty-five? Pretty; fair hair caught back in
a protective hood; a career woman who had presumably found
this esoteric profession to her liking. Was he being chauvinistic
because he found that surprising? At any rate she wasn't intimi-
dated by rank.

She had given him an idea and he called her over to the
window where the missing pane of glass lay in jagged fragments
on the floor. 'I would like you to check both the gap and the
fragments of glass on the floor for blood.' He added, 'Human,
of course.' And she grinned.

It was at that moment that Kersey joined them. He looked at
Wycliffe. 'Something?'

'I think we've been led up the garden. There's no doubt that
Roger Kemp was murdered and I'm pretty sure that the break-in
this morning was staged.'

'Agnes and the boy?'

'Who else?' His manner changed abruptly. 'How long since
you've seen Crispin?'

'Not since we questioned him before lunch.'

Without another word Wycliffe turned away and hurried from the room.

The girl looked at Kersey. 'Does he often get like that?'

Wycliffe tried the kitchen but it was empty, the dining room where the interrogations had been held that morning, but there was no one there. He tried Agnes's room. A knock on the door was unanswered so he pushed it open and went in. The curtains were half-drawn and Agnes was sprawled on the unmade bed, asleep. She woke and looked at him uncomprehending. 'Is something . . . ?'

He snapped at her, 'I'm looking for Crispin.'

She sat up. 'I don't know—'

He dashed back to the hall, up the stairs and along the corridor to Crispin's room. The door was open and the room empty. Barely in his career had he been so near to panic. Isobel opened the door of her room looking scared. 'Has something happened?'

'I'm looking for Crispin.'

'I haven't seen him since—'

'Think! Where does he go when he wants to be on his own?'

The girl was becoming more agitated. 'Why, he goes up to his garden I suppose . . .'

Of course; it was obvious!

A couple of minutes later he was in his car; down the drive, across the bridge and up the steep slope of the cliff road. His car was fitted with a siren which he could not remember having used but he used it now, speeding along the waterfront and through the village. Then up the steep slope out of Porthendel with Kellycoryk woods on his left and the new houses on his right. St Endel Churchtown, the church tower, then a sharp left turn before he pulled up by the old farm gate mounted between the twin ornamental pillars of the northern drive.

How long was it since the evening when he and Helen had looked over that gate, deciding whether or not to trespass?

The lodge windows were shuttered but the door was slightly ajar and he threw it open. Inside the light was dim and it took a moment or two for his eyes to accommodate. It was a sizeable room; the floor consisted of slate slabs. He became aware of tools and what must be compost bins arranged against one of the walls; overall there was a rank smell of soil.

It was seconds later when he spotted Crispin seated on the floor in a far corner of the room, knees drawn up, hands clasped about them.

Wycliffe made an effort to speak calmly. 'I've been looking for you, Crispin.' The boy did not answer and Wycliffe went on, 'Do you think we could have some light?' He fiddled with the shutter of the nearest window and succeeded in releasing it.

Light flooded in. Crispin was seated on a little heap of plastic sacks. On the floor near him Coryk was asleep beside a couple of little earthenware bowls, one of which still held some milk. Also on the floor was an unwound, bloodstained bandage.

Wycliffe walked over to the boy; the cat, disturbed, looked up at him but showed no interest. Crispin's hand was unbandaged and Wycliffe saw small but ugly teeth marks in the fleshy part of the hand below the little finger. There was inflammation.

'You should have that attended to.'

It was as though Crispin's soft brown eyes seemed to become aware of him for the first time. 'He didn't mean to do it; he was very frightened.'

Wycliffe held out a hand, 'Let's get out of here.'

The boy came stiffly to his feet and as he did so a small pruning knife slid off the plastic sacks on to the floor. Wycliffe picked it up; the blade was razor sharp.

'What were you going to do with this?'

Crispin looked vague. 'I don't know.'

'How about Coryk?'

'He'll find his way back.'

In the car going back he asked one question. 'I'm not under arrest?'

Wycliffe said, 'Should you be?'

There was no reply.

Friday early evening

They were seated at the little table in an interview room at the police station. Wycliffe and Lucy Lane sat opposite the boy. Wycliffe had set his chair a little back from the table, nearer the door.

Crispin's hand had been freshly and professionally bandaged. His face seemed drained of whatever colour it had ever possessed but the dark eyes retained their serenity of expression making it impossible to guess at his thoughts.

Lucy Lane started the tape. 'This interview begins at 17.05 ... You have been advised to have legal assistance but refused ... Remember that you do not have to say anything but that what you do say will be recorded. You understand?'

'Yes.' The reply was firm but indifferent.

'I am going to ask you about the events of this morning.'

Wycliffe intervened. 'It has been explained to you that DI Kersey and DC Lanyon are interviewing your aunt next door?'

A curt affirmative and Lucy continued: 'At what time did you come downstairs and go into the library?'

'It must have been at about half-past three.'

'Was the door locked?'

'No.'

'Were there lights in the library?'

'Only the little lamp on my father's table. He was sitting there as though he had been working but I think he was asleep. Coryk was curled up amongst the papers as usual.'

'Did you expect to find your father there?'

'No, I thought he would have been asleep in the little side-room.'

'Think carefully before you answer this question: were you carrying a pistol?'

'Yes.'

'With what purpose?'

'To shoot my father.' The statement came in a level voice devoid of any emotion.

'Go on.'

'I walked over to his chair, his eyes were closed but he opened them as I bent over him. It was then that I shot him in the temple – the right temple. He slumped forward on to the table. Coryk was very frightened. He leapt off the table with a sort of howl. I grabbed him to take him to the little side-room until I could deal with him properly but I was still holding the pistol so I suppose I was clumsy, and he bit me.'

Crispin glanced down at his bandaged hand.

Although he had known, broadly, what to expect, Wycliffe still looked at the boy with incredulity. This mild-mannered young man had confessed to murdering his father in simple straightforward terms, not exactly as though it were a matter of no consequence but rather as though it had been the inevitable outcome of what had gone before.

'All right; what happened when Coryk bit you?'

The boy frowned as though in an effort of recollection. 'I think it was then that Agnes came in; she must have heard something.'

'Go on.'

'Well, first she said, "Give me the gun," and I did. Then she went and got a bandage to tie up my hand. After that she looked at Father.'

'And then?'

'She said, "I'll see to this. I'll call you when I want you."'

'So you left her there?'

'Yes.'

Lucy Lane turned to look at Wycliffe, her face expressive of helplessness and disbelief.

Wycliffe took over. 'What did you suppose your aunt was going to do?'

A small lift of the shoulders. 'She was going to try to cover things up like Father did when I shot Bridget and like he did when he killed Mother.'

'Did you want that?'

He looked vague, indifferent. 'It didn't matter; I knew that one day people would find out about me.'

'Does it matter to you now that they have?'

A momentary pause, then, 'I don't think so.'

'About the little pistol – you must have had it in your possession from the time you shot Bridget until you used it on your father. Where did you hide it?'

'In the Northern Garden, under a pile of sacks in the old lodge.'

'Right. Now, coming back to this morning; what happened when your aunt called you?'

For the first time he sounded irritated. 'You know what happened; she had tried to make it look as though Father killed himself and I had to pretend to break in and to cut my hand on the window . . . I'm not going over all that.'

Wycliffe looked at Lucy Lane and Lucy switched off the tape. 'This interview is suspended at 17.53.'

Wycliffe said, 'I think we could do with a break.'

Outside, Lucy Lane said, 'The shrinks are going to have a field day with him.'

Half an hour later they were back in the interview room, the arrangement as before. Lucy Lane performed the required rituals, Crispin, although he had been for refreshment, looked as though he had never moved from his chair.

Lucy Lane opened the questioning. 'Why did you want to kill your father?'

Crispin shifted uncomfortably then, with a deep sigh he said, 'I'd meant to do it for a long time.'

'But why?'

There was silence in the little room so that the traffic in the street below sounded louder and voices reached them from else-where in the building. For a long minute Crispin remained motionless, staring straight in front of him, trance-like; and when he spoke he could have been recounting a dream.

'It started the night my mother died . . . I woke up and heard sounds coming from my parents' room. Their door was open and their light was on. I went along the corridor and looked in. Clare was there and she and my father were lifting Mother on to the bed . . . There was nobody else in the house.'

Wycliffe could see in his mind's eye the boy creeping along the bleak unlit passage to peer uncomprehendingly at the scene being enacted in the brightly lit bedroom.

Only when it seemed that Crispin would not continue, he prompted, 'And then?'

The boy's eyes blinked rapidly and he turned to face Wycliffe. 'I went back to my room but I left the door open so that I could hear and look out if I heard anything . . . They were talking, and after a little I saw Clare go to her own room. Then every-thing was quiet . . .

'I waited a long time and then I decided to see for myself, but the door of my parents' room was shut and though there was a light under the door and I could hear low voices, I couldn't bring myself to go in or to knock . . .'

They gave him time before Lucy Lane asked, 'And in the morning?'

He seemed to be recovering from an experience which had

been relived with great intensity, returning to the here and now.

'Clare got breakfast, as she always did when Agnes was away, and I asked her about Mother. She said that Mother had been poorly in the night but that she was all right again.'

'Did you believe that?'

'Yes.'

'And when, that evening, you heard about the boating accident?'

There was no change in the boy's expression but his hands, resting on the table top, shifted uneasily. 'I don't know . . . I suppose I began to wonder . . .'

There was another longish interval during which Crispin seemed about to speak but did not; then he said, 'It was almost two years later when I discovered what he had done in Mayne's Closet . . . Then I knew.'

'You knew what?'

'That he had murdered my mother and that I had almost seen it happen.'

It was some time before the boy added, simply, 'It was then that I decided to kill him.'

Wycliffe spent a good part of that evening alone in the DI's office at the police station, listening to the tapes. At intervals he heard the clocks chiming in the city centre but the passage of time meant little to him. At one point a timid constable brought him a mug of tea and a sandwich from the canteen.

The Crispin Kemp interview had lasted altogether for almost two hours and during that time his aunt had been questioned in another cubicle. Wycliffe juggled with the tapes to bring back passages which seemed to him of special significance.

'I couldn't think how to do it; I mean I had no weapon . . . I kept saying to myself, almost every night, "I'll kill him!" But time went on and I did nothing . . . I think that I might never have done it.'

Wycliffe recalled the sheepish, almost apologetic look which accompanied those words.

'But then he married that woman . . . And I said, "Now, I'll kill them both!"'

A little later in the tape he was explaining, 'I remembered my uncle Francis talking about a pistol that they had played with as children, thinking it was a toy. He said that they had found it in a box in the junk room . . . It was still there, and there was a little box of ammunition . . . I thought it had been kept specially for me.

'I knew nothing about pistols but I cleaned it and tried it out in the woods . . .'

There was extreme weariness in his voice when he added, 'You know the rest.'

Another question; Lucy Lane speaking. 'Why did you drive the car with your stepmother's body in the back to Kellycoryk? What did you expect to happen?'

An interval, then, 'I didn't care what happened but I wanted him to suffer before it was his turn . . . I suppose I thought that if he had known so well what to do with my mother's body—' The voice choked on an excess of bitterness.

Wycliffe sat motionless for some time. It occurred to him that Crispin was apparently unaware of the expert opinion that his mother's death had been accidental; unaware, or dared not accept?

It was after nine and he had not listened to the Agnes Kemp tape. He ran through it as one might skim the pages of a novel. Only one question interested him: 'Did you shift your brother's body?'

'Yes.'

'Why?'

A brief pause then, 'He spent a lot of his time staring at the ceiling; I thought he might feel more at home that way than slumped on the table.'

Wycliffe thought he could detect the sneer behind her words.

Chapter Twelve

Saturday morning 15 May

A troubled night but Wycliffe fell asleep in the small hours and woke with the sun shining through the curtains. He felt confused, vaguely depressed; the morning-after.

With infinite care he extricated himself from the bed. Helen muttered something and turned over but did not wake.

Six-twenty. Ten minutes later, dressed but unwashed and unshaven, he was on the beach. Substantial waves, remnants of the storm, broke along the shore and a broad band of seaweed and marine jetsam marked the highest reaches of the tide. He admitted to himself that he was unreasonably anxious that John Harvey's door should open. And it did.

'Had a bloody night? Anyway, the coffee pot's gurgling nicely so come on in.'

They drank their coffee sitting not far from the open door. Julia's painting of the cove hung as usual on the whitewashed wall at the bottom of the stairs and, for reasons which he could not explain, Wycliffe began to feel more at ease with himself.

After a few exchanges he said, 'I suppose you are more or less up to date?'

Harvey nodded. 'Isobel was here last night.' He added after a pause, 'She's a strange girl and she was in a strange mood.'

But Wycliffe was preoccupied with the boy. 'We had two sessions with him yesterday evening and it was almost eight when we finished. He said he wanted to "get it over". He doesn't seem to realize that for him it's scarcely begun.'

There was an interval while they sipped their coffee and watched the waves breaking, then Wycliffe, with a total disregard for the rules, launched on a succinct summary of the tapes. It was an unloading, a catharsis. And he rounded it off. 'After nearly two hours of that I was asking myself – I am still asking myself – whether I listened to a young killer or the victim of a warped upbringing. Thank God it's no part of my job to decide.'

Harvey reached for the coffee pot and refilled their mugs. When they were settled again he said, 'After qualifying I did a year in psychiatry. It was more like a theological college, plenty of doctrine and not much substance. My guess is that when Crispin's case comes to court there will be no difficulty in finding experts to contradict each other all along the line.

'Not that it will make much difference; faced with a lad like Crispin, and the choice between prison and a secure hospital, the court will play safe and send him to the hospital.'

Harvey yawned. 'Our little Crispy will become a case for treatment. And it will all be played over again with a different cast when there's talk of letting him out.'

Wycliffe, feeling to some extent reassured, though guilty because he had used Harvey as a confidant, was anxious to change the subject. 'What do you think will happen at Kellycoryk?'

Harvey sat back in his chair. 'Yesterday I would have guessed that things might go on much the same for a while, until the place began to actually fall down.'

'But you've changed your mind?'

'As I told you, Isobel was here last night. She was uptight. It was obvious that she was distressed by all that had happened but there was more to it than that and in the end it came out. Agnes had been talking; with what motive, I don't know, but she pointed out to the girl that as her father had died intestate she and Crispin would inherit, but that almost certainly, Crispin would be debarred.'

Wycliffe said, 'Isobel, the new mistress of Kellycoryk.'

'Exactly, but I'm quite sure the idea had never entered her head until Agnes put it there.'

'How did she react?'

'She was very restrained but it was obvious that mixed in with her distress there was a sense of excitement, almost of elation, which she was doing her best to conceal.'

Harvey looked at him with a quirkish smile. 'An odd turn-up for the book, don't you think?'

Wycliffe was thinking that if Beasley, the lawyer, was right, the whole truth might prove to be even odder.

The lawyer had said, 'You are asking about Bridget's will. Unfortunately there is no will . . .'

'So who inherits?'

'As I see it the beneficiaries can only be Roger Kemp and his children.'

'But the children are not hers, they are his by a former marriage.'

'That doesn't affect the position . . .'

But these thoughts Wycliffe kept to himself. He had other things than the future of Kellycoryk to occupy his mind. The investigation would begin to wind down but the paperwork would increase.

When he arrived back at the cottage Helen was already downstairs. 'Can you manage another coffee?'

Over the ensuing months, involved sporadically, Wycliffe watched the case pursuing its tortuous path through the legal jungle. The papers did their best with stories that owed something to *The Fall of the House of Usher* and more to Agatha Christie. There was no indication that anybody at Kellycoryk had broken ranks to help them. In the end Harvey proved right, it was decided that Crispin was a case for treatment.

It was more than two years after their stay in the cove that Helen read him a couple of paragraphs from the *Western Gazette*:

'Coast and Country, the leisure company responsible for several major projects in recent years, has put forward plans for the development of Kellycoryk in Veryan Bay. The proposals include an hotel, a competition golf course, provision for fly-fishing in well-stocked waters, and facilities for water sports.

'Miss Isobel Kemp, chief executive of the company, and present owner of Kellycoryk, told our reporter that everything would be done to preserve the unique natural attractions of the area. At the same time the project would provide much-needed employment for local people.

'It may be recalled that two years ago Kellycoryk was tragically in the news in connection with the murders of Miss Kemp's father and stepmother.'

Wycliffe had in his mind a vivid picture of Isobel, staring straight into his eyes, holding his gaze. 'I want you to know that I hate this place; I've grown up hating it, and the way we live . . . Our lives have been dominated by Father's obsession. We are not like other people – we can't mix.'

Times had changed.